DOCTOR WHO—EARTHSHOCK

DOCTOR WHO
EARTHSHOCK

Based on the BBC television serial by Eric Saward by
arrangement with the British Broadcasting Corporation

IAN MARTER

No. 78
in the
Doctor Who Library

A TARGET BOOK

published by
the Paperback Division of
W. H. ALLEN & Co. Ltd

A Target Book
Published in 1983
By the Paperback Division of
W. H. Allen & Co. Ltd
A Howard & Wyndham Company
44 Hill Street, London W1X 8LB

First published in Great Britain by
W. H. Allen & Co. Ltd 1983

Printed and bound in Great Britain by
Hunt Barnard Printing Ltd, Aylesbury, Bucks.

ISBN 0 426 19377 6

Contents

1

Shadows

The towering cliffside resembled a gigantic human skull with the dark openings of caves gaping like empty eye-sockets and nostrils. High overhead, the sun cast deep ominous shadows over the wild precipice and huge birds of prey wheeled silently in the hot dry air. At the bottom of the wall of rock yawned a cavernous mouth overhung with bristling thorn bushes and dangerously loose scree. Ten tall, lean figures were positioned in a menacing arc round the cave entrance, their young faces alert but impassive. They all wore tight-fitting green uniforms consisting of a kind of battledress tunic, trousers tucked into boots, a protective helmet and gloves. They stood motionless, levelling sleek tubular weapons into the darkness.

Behind them, other uniformed figures were huddled round a quietly humming machine resembling a small radar apparatus. They were staring intently at the greenish glow of a display screen which was protected by a hooded visor from the glaring sunlight. A pair of dish-shaped antennae connected to the machine were scanning slowly back and forth along the base of the cliff. Nearby, a rather plain plumpish woman in her late thirties and dressed in tattered buff overalls and a white mining helmet was pacing agitatedly up and down, her hands twisting the ragged remains of a pair of gloves. She darted anxious glances repeatedly at the sky, at the cave and at the frowning faces round the scanner.

After a long silence the young trooper seated at the control console turned to the tall, dark-haired officer standing beside him.

'It's hopeless, Lieutenant Scott. There's nothing, absolutely nothing,' he reported, gesturing at the blank screen.

Lieutenant Scott glanced helplessly across at the endlessly pacing woman and fingered his moustache. Then he walked slowly over to her.

'I'm sorry, Professor Kyle, there's no sign of them,' he murmured.

The young woman bit her lip as she struggled to remain composed. She was blinking back the tears behind her sunglasses.

'Well . . . could they be shielded from your apparatus in some way?' she asked desperately, stopping and spreading her arms vaguely.

Scott shook his head. 'Only by a lead or alloy screen,' he replied. 'The scanner detects and focuses on the body's cardioneurological activity. It's specifically tuned to mammalian life. It's extremely reliable.'

Professor Kyle looked up at the slowly circling vultures. 'I just can't believe that they're all dead,' she said in a hollow voice. 'It seems such a senseless waste.'

Scott nodded. Then he turned briskly. 'Trooper Walters, make one final scan. Maximum amplification,' he ordered. He put his hand gently on the Professor's shoulder. 'Rest assured that we shall catch whoever is responsible for this outrage, Professor Kyle,' he added quietly as the scanner whirred into action again.

'They can't be far away,' the Professor replied bitterly. 'I radioed as soon as I got out of the main cavern.'

'And we came as fast as we could,' Scott said abruptly, his pale gray eyes searching the woman's dark lenses as if he were seeking some loophole in her story. He looked at her ashen face, streaked with dirt and a little dried blood. 'How many of you were there down there?' he suddenly demanded.

8

'Eight including myself,' she answered in a startled voice.

'And what were you doing exactly?'

'A survey . . . I told you . . .' the Professor stammered, glancing nervously at the slowly tracking antennae. 'The inner cave system has only recently been discovered and it's unusually rich in fossils. Some of them are of hitherto unknown species and . . .'

'Palaeontologists?' Scott interrupted.

'And geophysicists,' Miss Kyle nodded. 'The area is geologically rather unstable and we . . .'

'It is also a security zone,' Scott cut in harshly. 'You have permits, of course?'

The Professor took off her sunglasses. The pupils of her large brown eyes shrank in the sudden glare. 'Of course, Lieutenant,' she retorted, trying to meet his hard stare without flinching.

'It doesn't make sense,' Scott exclaimed, turning on his heel and walking back over to the scanner.

After a few minutes, Trooper Walters switched off and stood up. 'Scan completed, sir. Negative. There's no sign of life.'

Scott contemplated the blank screen for a moment, fiddling uneasily with the ends of his moustache. He became aware that Professor Kyle was staring at him with a new determination in her pale face. He turned authoritatively to the efficent-looking young female officer beside him. 'Sergeant Mitchell, prepare the squad. We're going in,' he snapped.

The troopers checked their radios and switched on the twin lamps fitted on either side of their helmets. Within a few seconds the well-disciplined taskforce was ready to enter the caves.

Scott had drawn Mitchell aside. 'What do you think of Kyle's story?' he asked her.

9

She glanced across at the Professor. 'I think it's the truth, sir — at least as far as she knows it.'

Scott grunted. 'We'll keep her up front where we can see her, just in case,' he murmured, then went over to Kyle. 'I am sorry to drag you down there again after what you've been through,' he said.

Professor Kyle shrugged. 'You'd never find the bodies without my guidance,' she replied, managing a brave smile. 'The inner cave system is completely uncharted.'

Scott nodded curtly. He beckoned a squat, tough-looking female trooper standing by the scanner. 'Snyder, you remain here with Walters,' he ordered. 'I want a constant scan. Inform me the instant you detect anything.'

With a jerk of the head Scott motioned Professor Kyle to lead the way and he and his squad followed her into the darkness.

At first they made rapid progress through the outer tunnels of the labyrinth, which twisted and turned as it bored deeper and deeper into the mountain. Subsidiary tunnels branched continually in every direction and at regular intervals Scott halted the squad and their sharp twin beams stabbed into the hollow blackness, revealing shiny snakelike strata and weird gargoyle formations in the rock. Faint marker lamps had been installed in the main tunnel by the Professor's survey team and as the troopers jogged along, their shadows coiled and flapped around them on the uneven walls like long-forgotten ghosts.

Not far away in the waiting darkness, two other shadowy forms — without any light or human bodies to project them — suddenly detached themselves from the cold damp gloom and flitted silently along, keeping watch and biding their time. It was as if the darkness had formed itself into two humanoid shapes, tall and slim, male and female, hairless and featureless, with heads like huge polished

10

black stones. Lithe and powerful, they effortlessly stalked the thirteen struggling humans through the echoing maze, keeping always just out of reach of the probing helmet lamps. When the taskforce paused they also paused, their enormous heads poised as if listening, and no sound of breathing disturbed the dank air around them. And when they moved on again they moved together as one being, as if knowing each other's very thoughts.

These black beings were the sentinels of the mountain and the vigilant guardians of the secret at its very heart . . .

Out in the blinding sunlight, Trooper Snyder was squinting into the visor and following the dogged progress of the thirteen fluorescent dots moving in close formation across the scanner screen. Trooper Walters was leaning against the hood, swigging water from a flask and craning up at the ominous birds still hanging high above them.

Suddenly Snyder leaned closer and put her arms around the edge of the visor to shut out more of the glare. 'Is that supposed to happen?' she exclaimed.

'What?' Walters said, trying to peer over her shoulder.

'It's gone now. There was a kind of flaring just there,' Snyder explained, indicating a place on the screen close to the slowly moving pinpoints representing Scott and his squad.

Walters thumped the side of the console. 'Probably ghosting,' he muttered scornfully. 'This contraption's ancient.'

'But the Lieutenant said it was . . .' Snyder broke off and they both stared wide-eyed at a blurred luminous patch which had suddenly appeared next to the group of moving blips. 'There it is again!' Snyder cried. 'I think we should warn them!'

Walters leaned over and adjusted some of the controls. The strange patch grew momentarily brighter and then faded to nothing again. He shook his head. 'Just

tetramagnetic echo,' he grunted. 'There's nothing there.'
He took another greedy swig at the flask.

Snyder wiped the sweat out of her eyes and shaded the
scanner with her arms again. 'Well, I don't like it,' she
murmured, peering into the visor. 'I believe in ghosts.'

Adric lay on his bunk staring up at the ceiling. He was a
small wiry boy in his early teens, with a round face, wide
mouth and slightly snub nose, and his straight black hair
was cut across in a fringe. He wore a dull-coloured shirt
with a yellow jerkin over the top and his muddy-coloured
trousers were tucked into boots. On his chest was pinned a
large gold-edged badge in the shape of a star. His face was
crumpled in a sullen frown.

Adric was bored. Bored with the TARDIS. Bored with
the Doctor and his endless exploits. Bored with those
prattling females Tegan and Nyssa. Bored with himself. He
glanced in disgust around his room, bright with wallcharts
and complex three-dimensional puzzles, and all at once
appeared to make a decision. He sat bolt upright. 'I want to
go back,' he said aloud. 'I definitely want to go back.'

'Before you go anywhere you ought to read this!'
exclaimed the tall fair-haired young man who at that
moment had burst in through the door excitedly waving a
book at him. His face was long and tanned, and although
it was gentle it also suggested enormous strength and
determination. The cheerful newcomer was dressed in a
kind of pale, knee-length blazer with bright red edging, a
cream shirt, a cricket pullover and striped trousers. On
the open collar of the shirt two red question-marks were
embroidered. He looked as though he were dressed for a
summer garden party or a regatta.

Adric swung his legs off the bunk. 'What ought I to read,
Doctor?' he demanded resentfully.

The Doctor looked a trifle disconcerted, but his blue eyes

12

still sparkled with gentle enthusiasm. 'What's the matter Adric?' he inquired quietly, sitting on the edge of the bunk.

'I'm fed up, Doctor. I'm tired of being teased.'

The Doctor smiled. 'Everyone gets teased sometimes,' he pointed out reasonably.

'But you don't take me seriously,' Adric protested. 'You always answer all Nyssa's and Tegan's questions, but you never seem to bother with mine. How can I learn if you never have time to explain?'

The Doctor spread his long arms wide. 'I promise I'll make more time in future,' he said apologetically and then chuckled at his little joke.

Adric sprang angrily to his feet and walked furiously up and down his room. 'Oh very funny,' he cried. 'You've said that before, but something always interferes or you get us all into some scrape or other.'

The Doctor stood up, his face flushing. 'That's not fair!' he objected, turning away as if to hide his hurt feelings.

Adric faced him squarely. 'Oh no, it's never your fault when things go wrong, is it?' he retorted sarcastically.

'Have you quite finished?' asked the Doctor in a cold whisper.

'No, I haven't,' shouted Adric. 'There's lots more.'

'Well, it can wait!' snapped the Doctor striding to the door.

Adric followed hard on his heels. 'Well, I *can't*,' he cried, clasping the Doctor's arm. 'I'm sick of being an outsider. I want to go back. To my own people.'

The Doctor turned with his hand gripping the door knob and stared at the fuming boy in disbelief. 'Absolutely not!' he shouted after a moment's pause, wrenching open the door and striding out. 'I will not do it, Adric.'

'But you've done it before . . .' Adric pleaded, following him and almost running in order to keep pace.

'The TARDIS is not designed for E-Space,' the Doctor

13

argued, opening another door and bursting into the TARDIS control chamber. 'You tell him, Nyssa.'

An aristocratic-looking girl with a pale face framed by thick curls of brown hair looked up from the hexagonal console located in the centre of the softly humming chamber. She was dressed in a full-sleeved plum-coloured blouse and matching slacks. She looked startled. 'What?' she exclaimed, laying aside some galactic charts she had been examining.

'This young idiot wants to go home!' the Doctor exploded, finally managing to shake off Adric's tenacious grasp.

'That would mean putting the TARDIS into E-space,' Nyssa said gravely. 'It would be very dangerous. The Doctor's right.'

The Doctor was walking round and round the console, his hands thrust obstinately into the depths of his pockets. 'It's another universe. It's out of the question!' he muttered.

Adric faced them defiantly. 'I could easily plot a safe course,' he argued.

The Doctor stopped in his tracks. 'We'd have to pass through the CVE,' he cried, with a mocking laugh. 'Random negative co-ordinates, young man.'

Adric shook his head. 'The Monitor on Logopolis indicated that they were compatible,' he retorted with an appealing glance at Nyssa, begging for support.

The Doctor set off round the chamber again. 'You're not as bright as the Monitor, and even if you were I am not taking you back into E-Space,' he said dismissively.

'Then I'll find someone who will take me,' shouted Adric petulantly.

'Pop outside and hail a taxi then,' scoffed the Doctor.

There was a long silence. Then at last someone spoke.

'Is it really so dangerous, Doctor?' asked a nasal

14

Australian voice tentatively. The speaker was a red-haired, pretty girl a little older than Nyssa, who had been listening hard and trying to follow the argument. The girl was wearing a smart purple uniform blouse and skirt and stylish shoes. She had an efficient and determined air, but at the moment she was out of her depth. Her name was Tegan.

Instead of replying the Doctor muttered something indistinct about tiresome humanoids and sublime ignorance.

Adric calmed down a little. 'Romana is still in E-Space,' he said. 'Once I've calculated the course I'm sure she'll help me. Can I borrow the computer, Doctor?'

The tall figure waved his arms despairingly. 'Help yourself, Adric,' he muttered quietly, crossing to the console and busying himself with making adjustments to the TARDIS's complex navigational instruments. 'But don't expect the rest of us to wait around while you compute your own destruction . . .'

The Doctor's grim warning seemed to cast a chill in the air and Tegan and Nyssa exchanged concerned glances as Adric went over to the computer panel and eagerly set to work.

As the taskforce led by Lieutenant Scott penetrated deeper and deeper into the mountain, the going had grown steadily tougher and they had reached a section of low narrow tunnel which forced them to crawl painfully forward on their stomachs.

'Are you sure this is the only way down?' Scott panted in the stale clammy air, mopping his streaming face.

Professor Kyle nodded, gulping gratefully from Sergeant Mitchell's proferred water flask and hoping no one would notice her trembling hands. 'We had problems right from the start,' she gasped, trying unsuccessfully to sound casual. 'Tools disappearing. Then vital equipment mysteriously smashed. Things like that.'

'Sounds like sabotage to me,' Scott said loudly. 'Nothing mysterious about that.'

Professor Kyle wiped her scratched, dirty face with her rough sleeve. 'Sabotage? But who? Why?'

'What was that?' Scott murmered, suddenly turning his head and directing his twin helmet lights along a gully leading off at right angles from the main tunnel. 'Something seemed to move.'

The squad stirred uneasily, following Scott's powerful beams with wary eyes, their laser tubes poised to fire.

'Nothing there now, sir,' Sergeant Mitchell said after a hushed pause.

Scott shook his head as if to clear his vision. 'I'm sure something moved down there,' he insisted, with a long searching look at Kyle. She shrugged and said nothing.

They waited in the oppressive silence broken only by echoing drips. Eventually Scott motioned Professor Kyle to lead onward. After they had crawled for several hundred metres the tunnel widened and grew higher again. The taskforce pressed on, crouching and slithering precariously over the treacherously uneven and slippery floor. They had not gone far when the tunnel lighting suddenly flickered several times and then went out completely. Shouts of alarm and then a piercing scream rang out. A weird electrical crackle buzzed in the air and after a few seconds the faint lights came on again.

Scott slithered across the tunnel to an injured female trooper who was lying moaning in agony, her body unnaturally crooked and her face streaked with blood.

'I'm sorry, Lieutenant. It's my shoulder . . .' she gasped, as two troopers came to her aid.

Scott flicked on his radio, called up Walters and Snyder and told them to prepare to receive a casualty on the surface.

As he spoke, the communicator was suddenly flooded

16

with harsh static. The tunnel lights flickered uncertainly and the air was again filled with the strange buzzing.

'What's going on down there?' Walters voice broke faintly through the interference. 'The scanner's flaring like crazy up here.'

'See if you can get a fix on the source,' Scott ordered.

'It seems to be right next to you, Lieutenant,' Walters reported excitedly, 'but I can't get anything from the computer. It doesn't seem to register the flaring at all.'

Scott glanced at his squad. Some of them had removed their helmets and were touching their hair in amazement as they received a very mild kind of electric shock.

'The flare's disappeared now, sir,' said Walters as the static noise faded and the tunnel lights stopped flickering.

'Damn!' Scott muttered. 'If only we could get a fix on whatever's causing it . . .'

Professor Kyle had been clutching Sergeant Mitchell's arm and staring wildly about her. She was trembling and her lips moved, but at first no sound emerged. 'That noise . . .' she managed to whisper eventually in a haunted voice, 'I remember now . . . I heard it just before . . .'

'When?' Scott demanded.

Kyle shuddered, as if she were recalling some terrible nightmare from the past. 'Just a few seconds before we were attacked . . .' she blurted out in a choked voice.

Deeper in the dark labyrinth a strange commotion suddenly disturbed the deathly silence. A harsh scraping and whirring noise was accompanied by a shivering in the rock walls as a faint blinking yellow light appeared. It grew brighter and brighter, and with a final series of raucous shrieks a battered blue police box materialised, faded, reappeared and fell silent. The darkness seemed to gather itself like a dense cluster of swirling black drapery and then to settle itself to wait . . .

Inside the brightly lit control chamber of the TARDIS the Doctor gave the time-warp anchorage unit a final pat to encourage stability and flashed a smile of satisfaction at his three young companions. 'Here we are again!' he announced in a jaunty tone.

'Where?' demanded Tegan, exchanging sceptical glances with Nyssa.

'Earth, of course. Where else?' the Doctor replied blandly. Nyssa's fine features wrinkled with disappointment. 'Not again,' she sighed.

'Twenty-sixth century,' Adric murmered, frowning at the computer. 'AD 2526 actually,' he added helpfully for Tegan's benefit.

'Not a bad vintage at all,' remarked the Doctor cheerfully, operating the switch to raise the shutter covering the external viewer screen.

'Why Earth?' Nyssa asked disapprovingly.

'Why on earth not?' the Doctor joked, studying the viewer with childlike pleasure. 'Adric wants to use the computer, I want to take a little walk.'

'In the dark?' Tegan exclaimed, pointing unenthusiastically at the screen.

'Doctor, since your regeneration you've become decidedly immature,' Adric remarked acidly without looking up from his calculations.

The Doctor's mild face abruptly clouded with rage and for a few dangerous moments it looked as though he would erupt. Controlling himself with great difficulty he operated the external door lever. Then he reached into his pocket and drew out what looked like a parchment scroll tied with a scarlet ribbon. With a deft flicking movement he unrolled it and shook it into shape. It was a flexible straw panama hat with a red band. With exaggerated dignity the Doctor put it on his head. He strode to the open door and turned. 'I might be back . . .' he said haughtily and then stalked outside.

For a moment no one spoke. Then Tegan walked quietly out after him.

'It's all got rather silly, hasn't it?' Nyssa said loftily.

'I didn't mean to be so rude,' Adric mumbled shame-facedly.

Nyssa went over and put her arm round his shoulder. 'When you've completed your calculations we'll show them to the Doctor,' she said encouragingly. 'When he's calmed down I'm sure we'll be able to persuade him . . .'

Adric worked away in silence for a few seconds and then looked up gratefully. But Nyssa had gone. He was quite alone.

2

Labyrinth of Death

Trooper Walters brushed the sweat from his eyes as he concentrated on the softly glowing monitor. Two fluorescent spots representing the wounded trooper and her escort returning to the surface were moving laboriously in one direction, while a tight cluster of eleven dots showing the painful progress of the taskforce moved slowly the opposite way, deeper into the mountain.

Suddenly three new pinpoints appeared one after another to one side and a short distance ahead of the advancing squad. One of the new blips was pulsing oddly. Walters stared at it intently and then gasped in astonishment.

'What is it?' Snyder said, running over to the scanner.

Walters flicked on his radio. 'Lieutenant Scott — three unidentified mammalian life-forms just registered in your vicinity,' he rapped, 'and I know it's impossible, sir, but one of the blips is ectopic.'

'Meaning what?' crackled Scott's voice impatiently.

There was a short pause while Walters glanced at Snyder.

'Meaning that . . . that one of the sources must have two hearts!' Walters replied uncertainly.

There was another pause. The radio crackled and hissed.

'Have you been drinking, Walters?' Scott demanded.

Trooper Snyder leaned over and confirmed the scanner observation while Walters ran a rapid series of computer checks.

'The computer confirms it, sir,' Walters reported at last.

'Aliens!' Scott's metallic voice rang out eerily against the cliff.

'At least one, sir.'

'Quick, give me a fix on them,' Scott snapped.

Walters read off a long string of co-ordinates from the computer and then listened while Scott and Kyle conferred.

Then the Lieutenant spoke hurriedly. 'Listen, Walters, the Professor estimates that the alien, or aliens, or whatever, must be in one of the fossil caves near where she and her team were attacked. We're going in right now. Keep your eyes on that monitor.' The radio clicked off.

There was silence and then Snyder jabbed her finger at the two lonely blips struggling towards the surface. 'I don't like it. They're hardly moving,' she murmured, unhitching her laser tube. 'I'm going down to help . . .'

Before Walters could object, the dumpy little figure had been swallowed up by the dark maw gaping hungrily at the foot of the vast cliff.

Guided by Walters via the radio, Trooper Snyder crept quickly along the dimly lit tunnels to rendezvous with the wounded trooper and her escort. Every so often she stopped to listen and thought she heard their scuffling steps somewhere in the gloomy honeycomb ahead, but her tentative calls received no response. Eventually, as she emerged from the low narrow section and scrambled to her feet, she heard a faint voice.

'Is that you, Snyder?' it called.

'Yes. Wait there for me,' she shouted thankfully, quickening her pace.

'Who's that with you?' cried the voice.

Snyder stopped dead. She tried to shout that she was alone, but her throat had shrunk tight and her lips felt dry as dust.

At that moment Walters' voice burst through a mush of static on her receiver. 'You're very close now, Snyder, but there's a lot of flaring near you. Can you see anything yet?'

'Nothing,' she managed to croak. She tugged off her helmet and felt her hair suddenly bristle in the fizzing air.

'The flare's increasing and it's getting closer to you,' Walters hissed barely distinctly, 'but it's just like last time, I can't get a reading on the computer . . .'

'Snyder!' yelled the voice from along the tunnel. 'What are you two playing at? You're both crazy . . . You're . . .' The words stretched out into a long series of shrill, bloodcurdling screams, and then there was silence.

For several seconds Snyder was rooted to the spot. Then she started to run towards the terrible sound, charging and priming her laser as she ran. Rounding a corner, she came upon two dim shapes standing in the shadows. She froze. Then a relieved laugh burst from her. 'You really scared me,' she cried, 'I thought you were . . .'

'Snyder . . . Snyder come out of there . . . They're both dead,' Walters was screaming from the radio. 'That flare just wiped them out and now it's right on top of you. Come back . . .'

Something splashed over Snyder's boots. Tearing her eyes away from the two ghostly apparitions, she glanced down. What she saw made her stomach fly up into her throat. She was standing in a shallow pool of steaming, viscous liquid in which were floating the scorched and tattered uniforms of two troopers. A sickly smell hung in the crackling air.

Snyder tried to back away, fumbling with her laser as she stared mesmerised at the two black mummy-like figures, their polished, featureless faces watching her and their left arms slowly rising to point accusingly at her. The tips of their outstretched hands suddenly exploded in a searing flash. Snyder's empty uniform collapsed into a puddle of sticky oozing froth and floated beside her radio while Walter's panic-stricken pleas broke intermittently through the static.

The two shadows waited motionless for a moment, as if listening to Walters' desperate, disembodied voice. Then they spun round and darted silently away towards the interior.

Nyssa and Tegan had joined the Doctor in the cavern outside the TARDIS and had been trying to win him round. 'Just breathe deeply and slowly and relax. It's easy,' Tegan was suggesting.

'All right,' the Doctor agreed reluctantly, 'but I refuse to risk taking that young fool into E-Space just so that he can resume his criminal activities among the less savoury inhabitants of Terradon.' He stood still and took several deep breaths. 'I like it here, it's so peaceful and cool,' he murmured happily.

'It's stuffy and damp . . .' Tegan began.

Nyssa frowned her into silence and took the Doctor's arm. 'At least look at Adric's calculations,' she gently pleaded.

The Doctor considered a moment. 'Oh I'll look at them. But I don't promise anything.'

'No, of course not,' Nyssa agreed with a quick grin at Tegan, who came up and took the Doctor's other arm.

'Now let's take that little walk,' Tegan suggested, 'and then you can go back and apologise to Adric.'

Before the Doctor could react to her ill-timed suggestion, Tegan suddenly exclaimed: 'There's something wrong here. If we are underground it should be pitch dark, but it isn't, Doctor.'

The Doctor laughed and ran his hand along the cavern wall as they walked. 'Phosphorescent salts deposited by

23

hypervolcanic gases,' he explained, showing them his glittering fingertips.

'And something else,' Nyssa said, peering across at the opposite wall in the bluish twilight. 'Look, Doctor. Bones!'

There, inlaid in the iridescent glassy rock, were enormous fossilised bones. Some were detached and jumbled together while others were still connected at the joints to form the partial skeletons of gigantic animals.

Tegan felt along the thick curving protuberances of a huge ribcage. 'It's like a big graveyard,' she whispered in awe.

'Fascinating. What an amazing species . . .' the Doctor murmured almost reverently, gazing in wonder at the ancient remains.

'Dinosaurs?' Tegan exclaimed.

'Were they your ancestors, Tegan?' Nyssa asked.

Tegan gave a hollow laugh. 'I hope not, sport,' she retorted. 'Most of them had a brain the size of a pea.'

'But you should be proud of such magnificent forebears,' the Doctor chided her. 'They were the most successfully adapted species ever. Their fossilised remains are found scattered over the entire planet! Rather impressive for creatures with pea-sized brains.' The Doctor smiled benevolently at Tegan and then wandered further round the cavern fingering the fossils thoughtfully. 'They survived for a hundred million years and yet they died out almost overnight,' he said in a hushed voice.

'How?' Nyssa demanded sceptically.

'First hypothermia, then starvation.'

'Caused by what?'

'The Earth collided with something,' the Doctor explained.

'An asteroid?' Nyssa suggested.

The Doctor looked slightly shamefaced. He did not reply immediately but squatted down and started sketching something in the thick dust with his finger. 'Possibly,' he said at last. 'I'm afraid I don't actually know. I keep meaning to pop back and see, but I never seem to get the time . . .'

'It's impossible,' Tegan objected, watching as the Doctor drew a diplodocus with enormous tail and endless neck. 'It couldn't have wiped them all out at once.'

The Doctor drew a tiny sticklike human to scale with his dinosaur. 'Whatever it was, the impact would have thrown billions of tonnes of earth and rock into the atmosphere, enveloping the entire planet,' he replied.

'The sunlight would have been blocked for years and years,' Nyssa added pensively.

'Exactly,' the Doctor resumed. 'The surface of the Earth would have cooled catastrophically. Without warmth reptiles cannot function, and without sunlight their food cannot grow.'

Tegan suddenly shivered. The cavern was decidedly chilly. 'When did all this happen?' she demanded, still not quite convinced.

'About sixty-five million years ago,' the Doctor answered, standing upright and listening intently for a moment.

Tegan grinned at Nyssa. 'I wonder what my real ancestors were up to at the time,' she giggled.

The Doctor frowned. 'Oh, they were at an even more primitive evolutionary stage than you are . . .' he murmured, setting off stealthily towards the mouth of a tunnel at the end of the cavern.

Tegan glanced down at the scuffed remains of the Doctor's sketch. 'Poor old dinosaur,' she muttered with genuine feeling. Then with a glance back at the TARDIS she hurried after the Doctor and Nyssa.

In the humming warmth of the TARDIS, Adric was bent

over the computer concentrating on a long and complex series of calculations. Occasionally he glanced up at the viewer screen, which showed his three friends deep in conversation somewhere outside. 'At least they don't seem to be fighting,' he murmured, keying a number of co-ordinates into the computer.

A sudden movement caught his eye as the trio moved away. He reached over and set the viewer on automatic tracking. 'Don't stray too far, will you,' he muttered scornfully, 'because I don't want to have to come and get you out of trouble.' He sat watching them for a few seconds, his thoughts wandering. Flashes of memory recalling some of the scrapes he had got involved in since that fateful day he had stowed away in the TARDIS and memories of his home planet and of his dead brother came surging into his mind. He almost gave way to tears as the images crowded in on him.

Then he pulled himself together and turned back to his lonely task at the keyboard . . .

Sensing that the alien prey was not far from his grasp, Lieutenant Scott urged his tiring squad forward, deeper and deeper into the mountain. Professor Kyle had been a hindrance, struggling along obviously still in a state of shock after the attack on her colleagues earlier. But she was an indispensable guide in the confusing maze where many of the marker lights were damaged or missing. She had been gasping and stumbling pitifully for some time. Suddenly she pitched forward onto her face and lay groaning.

'I'm sorry . . . I just can't keep up . . .' she panted.

Scott reluctantly ordered a brief rest. Sergeant Mitchell helped the Professor to sit up and gave her water. With lasers primed, the troopers covered the gaping tunnels surrounding the squad.

Scott's communicator bleeped and Walters' terrified voice echoed around them. 'Snyder and the other two have disappeared off the scanner, sir. There was a flare next to them and their blips just vanished,' he cried.

Scott exchanged horrified glances with Mitchell. 'Calm down, Walters. Have you checked for faults?' he demanded, trying hard to sound logical.

'I ran a complete check, Lieutenant. I know this thing's old, but there's no malfunction,' Walters replied. There was a brief pause, then Walters added: 'There's no other explanation. They must be dead.'

The troopers looked at one another and gripped their lasers more firmly.

'The aliens . . .' Scott breathed.

'No, sir,' Walters crackled on, 'they've hardly moved. They're still *ahead* of you. But Snyder and the others were only a few hundred metres from the surface.'

'It must be the aliens,' Scott snapped into his transmitter. 'What else could it be?'

Professor Kyle wiped her filthy face with a tattered glove. 'Some of the tunnels are unstable . . . there have been rockfalls,' she said weakly. 'Or perhaps they hit a gas pocket . . .'

Sergeant Mitchell stepped smartly forward. 'Let me take two troopers and double back, sir,' she suggested. 'At least we can help cover your rear.'

Scott hesitated. Then with a curt nod he agreed. Mitchell selected a pair of crack personnel from the squad and set off rapidly back the way they had come.

Scott pulled Kyle rather roughly to her feet. 'I'm sorry Professor, but we must press on at once. People's lives are at stake.'

Professor Kyle swallowed hard. 'Of course. I can manage . . .' she murmured bravely. 'We are almost at the main cavern now.'

Scott spoke rapidly into his radio. 'This is our final push, Walters. I want to know the moment you see anything on that contraption of yours. You hear me? *Anything*.'

They pushed forward with renewed vigour, following the steeply sloping tunnel at a sharp angle downwards. Their headlamps began picking out the phosphorescent flecks in the tunnel walls as they descended into the heart of the mountain. Soon the tunnel levelled out and they suddenly found themselves entering a large, lofty cavern. Its walls were marbled with beautifully coloured strata and twisting veins of mineral deposits, and pockmarked with weird knobbly fossil fragments. A battery of working lights hung from the roof and an assortment of excavating and surveying equipment was scattered around the cave floor. In the centre of the cavern a small drilling rig had been erected. Most of the equipment was damaged or lying about in pieces and few of the overhead lights were functioning properly.

Professor Kyle hesitated in the entrance. 'This is the main chamber . . .' she whispered nervously, shrinking back against the wall.

'So this is where you were attacked,' Scott murmured, signalling to his squad to make a quick recce round the huge cavern. 'There don't appear to be any bodies, Professor,' he added suspiciously.

Kyle was staring into the far corner. 'There's been another rockfall . . .' she murmured.

A trooper hurried over and reported that nothing had been found.

'So where are these aliens?' Scott muttered, advancing very cautiously towards the middle of the chamber.

The Professor pointed to several dark openings on the far side. 'They must be in one of those smaller subsidiary caverns,' she said in a barely audible whisper, her face white as chalk under the grime and dried blood. 'Yes . . . I think the attack came from there.'

Within seconds Scott had disposed his troopers in concealed positions around the chamber. He grabbed Kyle's arm and dragged her behind the rockfall. Then he called up Walters. 'What are they doing now?' he asked in an undertone.

'The aliens are just moving off again,' Walters reported. 'They're closing with you rather fast, sir.'

Scott nodded with satisfaction. 'We're ready for them whoever they are,' he breathed, charging his laser tube, his grey eyes alive with anticipation. 'Now I don't want to give myself away, Trooper Walters, so maintain strict radio silence from now on . . .'

Meanwhile, Sergeant Mitchell and her two-man detachment were just approaching the low narrow section of the main tunnel. For some time they had felt a curious tingling sensation in their scalps and had been aware of a hidden presence stalking them. The tunnel lights were flickering spasmodically. Suddenly they died completely. The three troopers edged forward, sweeping the tunnel with their sharp parallel helmet-beams.

All at once one of them slithered and almost fell. There was a sinister sucking and squashing sound as he regained his balance. He looked down and gave a shuddering gasp of horror, covering his mouth with his gloved hand. The remains of three uniforms floated at their feet.

Mitchell bent down and peered at an identity flash still attached to a scorched sleeve. 'Snyder . . .' she breathed. The flashes on the other two uniforms had been burnt away.

'What kind of weapon could do *that*?' one of them gasped.

Just then, Walters broke through the static on Mitchell's radio. 'Can you see anything . . . anything at all? The flaring's right on top of you now!'

29

Mitchell calmly charged her laser. 'Nothing yet,' she muttered, 'but I don't think we have long to wait.'

There was a long silence, broken only by the buzzing of the radio. Then a splinter of loose rock clattered somewhere along the tunnel behind them. They whipped round. Two tall silhouettes were advancing steadily towards them, their smooth black bodies totally absorbing the sharp beams of the troopers' lamps.

'There are two of them,' Mitchell whispered into her transmitter. 'We have them covered. They're not armed. They're not even . . .'

At that moment Walters burst in incredulously, but his words were unintelligible. Mitchell dropped the radio and it sank into the mess at her feet.

Still approaching, the two figures raised their left arms. There was a brilliant flash and one of the troopers disappeared, his empty uniform slumping into a steaming puddle. Mitchell and the other man fired their lasers simultaneously, but the deadly rays had no effect; they were simply absorbed by the advancing shadows. Mitchell started screaming hysterically, still firing her laser. There were two more quick flashes and two more uniforms collapsed smoking into the gluey pool.

At once the two figures turned and sped away in the direction from which they had come. The three parallel beams from the scattered helmets of the three victims criss-crossed the darkness like searchlights in a silent night sky.

3

Uneasy Allies

Nyssa and Tegan had been warily following the Doctor as he led the way cautiously along the tunnel leading from the cave where the TARDIS had materialised. Before long the tunnel opened out into the large central cavern.

The Doctor stopped in the entrance. 'Wait. I have a feeling we shouldn't go any further,' he warned them.

'It looks like some kind of mine,' Tegan whispered, pointing to the drilling rig.

'I can't see anyone . . .' murmured Nyssa.

'Stay just where you are!' rapped a cold, efficient voice. Lieutenant Scott stepped out from behind the rockfall and then the rest of his squad appeared with weapons levelled menacingly.

'What's going on?' Tegan demanded aggressively, quickly recovering from her astonishment.

The Doctor laid a restraining hand on her arm. 'Good morning . . . or is it afternoon . . . or even evening?' he said amiably, stepping forward with hand outstretched.

Scott waved his laser. 'Stay just where you are!' he snapped.

'I am the Doctor and these are my two young friends Nyssa and Tegan,' the Doctor persisted. But he was silenced by the sudden whirr of Scott's laser charging up.

'Do you recognise any of them, Professor?' Scott inquired as Kyle emerged from her hiding place behind the rocks.

She shook her head, obviously very relieved.

'Indeed no. We haven't had the pleasure . . .' the Doctor

couldn't help gallantly remarking, doffing his hat with a friendly smile.

At that moment, Scott's communicator bleeped urgently. In a faint, toneless voice Walters reported that Sergeant Mitchell and the two troopers had been killed. A murmur of outrage and horror ran through the squad.

'Order!' Scott barked. There was immediate silence. 'Did you pick anything up,' he asked Walters.

'Just the same flaring, sir, but Sergeant Mitchell reported encountering two hostiles.'

Lieutenant Scott eyed the three strangers in front of him. 'Human?' he asked.

'She didn't say, sir. She just said they weren't armed.'

At a sign from Scott, a couple of troopers gave the three suspects a quick but thorough search. 'Nothing, sir,' they reported.

Scott looked baffled. For a moment he was silent. 'Have you still got that flaring?' he asked at last.

'No, it disappeared, sir, but I'm still getting that freak signal — the ectopic blip.'

'Oh yes, the freak signal. I think I know where *that's* coming from,' Scott muttered dangerously, staring hard at the self-possessed young man dressed in carnival clothes who had introduced himself as 'the Doctor'.

The young man took a few steps towards the Lieutenant. 'I assure you that we know nothing about the deaths of your men,' he said earnestly, 'but can we do anything to help?'

Scott grabbed the Doctor by his lapels and flung him brutally against the rocks. Nyssa and Tegan attempted to rush the Lieutenant, but they were instantly restrained.

'Seven innocent people were murdered in this chamber,' Scott snarled, yanking the Doctor back to his feet. 'Where are their bodies?'

Nyssa and Tegan started to protest, but Scott turned on them savagely. 'Don't waste my time,' he cried. Then he thrust his laser roughly against the Doctor's throat. 'Where have you hidden the bodies?' he repeated.

Professor Kyle had been looking on with mounting distress. Much as she wanted the murderers of her colleagues brought to justice, she found the Lieutenant's methods distasteful. 'The rockfall . . . The bodies could be under there!' she exclaimed hopefully.

Scott's eyes gleamed with victory. He jabbed the laser into the Doctor's ribs and began forcing him over towards the huge mass of jagged boulders and scree. 'Under the rockfall?' he said quietly. 'Shall we take a look, "Doctor"?'

With a semicircle of laser tubes covering them at point-blank range, the Doctor, Tegan and Nyssa were compelled to struggle with the heavy stones. They had been toiling away for some time when the big flat rock Nyssa was throwing all her modest weight behind suddenly slid aside with a harsh grating noise. It revealed what looked like the corner of a heavy metallic hatch set into the base of the cavern wall.

'What's that?' Scott demanded, hurrying over.

Nyssa tapped it. It rang with a dulled echoing sound. 'I don't know,' she answered.

Scott glanced at the Doctor. He was staring at the metal corner suspiciously. The Lieutenant ordered his squad to help clear the remaining rocks away from the strange object. Somewhat confused, the troopers shouldered their lasers and set to work.

Professor Kyle had been watching the operation apprehensively. Suddenly something caught her eye among the boulders and she jumped onto the rockpile and started frantically tugging at them. After a few minutes she straightened up with something in her hand. 'Lieutenant Scott!' she cried in a shocked voice. 'Look!'

Scott and the Doctor clambered over to her. She was holding between two fingers the tattered remnants of an

33

overall similar to the one she herself was wearing. 'This . . . this belonged to my assistant . . . Doctor Kahn,' she informed them quietly, her voice tremulous with emotion.

Adric had become so engrossed in solving the complex equations that would enable him to calculate a course for his journey through E-Space that he had quite forgotten about his friends outside. When eventually he did look up at the viewer it was blank. The trio had vanished. '*Now* where have you got to?' he muttered exasperatedly.

Suddenly a piercing, high-pitched whine filled the TARDIS control chamber. Adric winced and clapped his hands tightly over his ears. The sound seemed to slice right through his body. In desperation he sprang up and darted round and round the main control console, peering at display panels and jabbing his fingers at touch buttons and switches. But it was no use. The unbearable noise persisted and soon Adric began to feel very very sick. 'Where . . . Where is it coming from?' he moaned.

The noise transformed itself into a penetrating throbbing which shook Adric so violently he began to fear that his flesh would be literally shaken from his bones . . .

Not far away, the two ghostly silhouettes were twisting effortlessly through the tunnels, unhindered by the darkness and with the air fizzing around them. Their secret was in danger and they must protect it. That was their sole function, their whole existence. Their systems were perfectly attuned. As they swiftly approached the cavern in the furthest depths of the mountain the interference in the TARDIS's mechanisms relentlessly increased.

The troopers and their three prisoners had soon cleared enough of the rockfall to reveal a heavy metallic plate, about a metre square, set into the foot of the cavern wall.

Scott examined it carefully for a moment and then went over to the Doctor.

'So this is your secret,' he said challengingly. 'For this you are prepared to kill innocent people in cold blood.'

The Doctor gestured helplessly. 'I have already explained — we know nothing about it,' he protested wearily.

'Listen, we're telling you the truth,' Tegan yelled into the Lieutenant's face.

Scott shoved her roughly aside and thrust his laser against the Doctor's neck. 'Open the hatch, Doctor!' he ordered.

'I can't!' shouted the Doctor.

The charging circuits inside the tube whirred menacingly and the Doctor froze and kept silent.

Nyssa stepped forward. 'I could try,' she offered.

'Stay where you are!' Scott rapped harshly. 'I want the Doctor to open it.'

At that moment there was a shout of panic from the other side of the chamber, followed by a fierce burst of laser fire. The group by the hatch spun round to see a trooper firing frantically into the mouth of the tunnel leading to the surface and backing away from something with a look of terrified disbelief, distorting his young face like a stocking mask. The working lights in the cavern roof dimmed and the air began to sizzle like hot fat. There was a brilliant explosive flash from the tunnel mouth, the trooper's weapon flew out of his hands and his uniform crumpled like an empty sack amid billows of rubbery smoke.

For an instant, the horrified onlookers were paralysed. Then Scott yelled an order and everyone took cover behind the rocks and abandoned equipment. Professor Kyle desperately squeezed herself into a niche near Scott, the Doctor and his two friends. She was visibly shaking as she stared at the two black figures which suddenly came

35

stalking into the cavern from the tunnel. They stopped and raised their left arms in front of them. A rapid staccato burst of searing flashes shot out of their hands and sent sharp splinters of rock showering over the hidden troopers.

'It's them . . . I remember now . . . the flash and the tingling . . . they came up behind us . . .' Kyle had begun to mutter.

'It was those things that attacked you?' Scott murmured. The Professor nodded. 'It all happened so very quickly . . .'

'Do you know why they attacked you?' the Doctor asked, watching the two figures move very slowly, with sinister gracefulness, into the centre of the huge cavern, then pause, their egglike heads swaying from side to side as if seeking out their prey.

Kyle shook her head. 'What in heaven's name *are* they?' she whispered incredulously.

'Androids,' the Doctor replied without hesitation. 'That's why they didn't register on your cardioneurological detector, Lieutenant.'

'Are they yours?' Scott asked, his voice a mixture of awe and suspicion.

The Doctor smiled ruefully. 'Certainly not, Lieutenant. You'll find that they will eliminate me just as readily as you or anyone else here.' The Doctor snatched off his hat and then straightened up very carefully in order to peer through a gap in the rocks that gave a better view of the creatures.

'But why attack us?' the Professor shrugged. 'There's no reason.'

'Oh yes, there's a reason all right,' the Doctor murmured with a frown, 'and whoever or whatever is controlling those creatures knows exactly what it is.'

The heads of the androids had tilted slightly back and they were now scanning slowly back and forth behind their outstretched arms.

36

Tegan shivered. 'It's just as if they were sniffing us out,' she breathed.

'I wonder whose bloodhounds they are?' the Doctor muttered grimly, chewing the brim of his had as he watched the macabre ballet in the middle of the cavern.

Somewhere just beyond the outer edges of the solar system, deep in the innermost recesses of a gigantic spacecraft, two silver figures were staring intently at a hazy three-dimensional image resembling a hologram. The image was being created at the focus of three telescopic projectors set at an angle to one another and all aligned towards the centre of a large disc suspended beneath them. The ghostly scene hovering above the disc was panning slowly to and fro and it showed the interior of a cavern strewn with rocks and scattered equipment.

One of the two silver figures was considerably larger than the other, but both resembled humans in having heads, torsos and limbs. The rigid mask-like faces had eyeless sockets and immobile mouth-like apertures, but no noses. They had no ears, but a network of wires and pipes connecting a bulging section on each side of their heads to a similar bulge on the top. The limbs were jointed like human ones, but were much thicker and more powerfully tubular, and the arms terminated in enormous hands like steel gauntlets. Tubes ran snaking over the hard metallic surfaces of their bodies from flat, box-like units protected by gratings which were fitted onto their chests. From these units there issued a continuous rhythmic hissing noise, almost like human breathing. Similar tubes led into a large cylindrical powerpack set across the back of their shoulders. A kind of control terminal was attached to their abdomens and heavy, blunt-nosed guns were clipped to the figures' belts.

In the darkness surrounding them, an array of weird

oscillating humming sounds accompanied a dancing tracery of indicator lights which flashed and pulsed over the walls.

The larger of the two figures reached out a bunched metal hand and made a small adjustment to the control module beneath the softly glowing disc. At once the reddish image under the projectors came to rest. The figure's rhythmic breathing paused momentarily and with a faint leathery creak it leaned forward to examine the outline of the mass of rocks. After a slight stirring of inner mechanisms, the figures spoke in a rasping, hollow, mechanical voice.

'They are there. They must be destroyed. Destroyed at once.' The huge hand hovered above a series of triggering buttons and then descended . . .

Once again the air in the cavern crackled and the lights dimmed as a fusillade of incandescent flashes burst from the oustretched hands of the two androids. The rocks sheltering the Doctor and the others shattered and flew apart and vicious razor-sharp fragments whipped in all directions. The troopers returned fire as best they could, but the laser pulses sank harmlessly into the creatures' seemingly indestructible bodies.

'Tell them to concentrate their fire!' the Doctor shouted into the Lieutenant's ear. 'Go for the male first — the centre of the chest.'

Scott yelled instructions and all the troopers aimed and fired simultaneously at the male. The creature raised its right arm to shield its body from the clustered rays. After a few seconds the arm glowed and then exploded in a shower of sparks. A triumphant cheer rippled among the hidden troopers as the female android seized the male's remaining arm and dragged the creature out of range behind a natural buttress, sending flash after flash ripping into the rocks to cover their retreat.

'How very touching,' the Doctor murmured grimly, 'they seem almost human, don't they?'

As soon as the androids had reached the safety of the buttress, near the mouth of the tunnel lending to the cave where the TARDIS had materialised, the uproar ceased abruptly. Nothing stirred. There was an eerie silence.

'We're trapped,' Scott muttered with a grimace. 'Those things can cover all the exits from there.' He flicked on his radio and tried to contact Walters, but no reply broke through the thick static buzzing from the receiver.

'Surely your friends will realise something's wrong down here?' Tegan said hopefully.

'Sooner or later,' Scott replied tersely.

Tegan glanced at Nyssa. 'Let's hope it's sooner!' she said, trying to sound casual, but feeling very frightened.

The Doctor peered through his spyhole again. 'They're just waiting for us to make a silly move,' he warned. 'I am sure they will attack again.' He crouched down and turned to Kyle. 'Professor, were you and your colleagues working near the rockfall when you were attacked?'

'Yes, Doctor, we were studying fracture deformation patterns,' Kyle replied timidly, nervously twisting her gloves.

'In that case you were virtually on top of that hatch we've uncovered,' the Doctor mused. 'Perhaps the androids are guarding it.'

'But why should they?' the Professor demanded distractedly.

The Doctor turned to Lieutenant Scott. 'I think we should try to find out,' he suggested.

Scott scratched his moustache. 'I haven't had much experience fighting androids,' he said doubtfully.

'Well, as I said just now, they're almost like humans,' shrugged the Doctor.

'Only androids function much more logically . . .' Nyssa added.

'. . . which is also their chief weakness,' continued the Doctor eagerly, 'and we can exploit that weakness, Lieutenant. I propose that we attack the hatch!'

Scott stared at the Doctor as though he were demented. 'That would only expose our own weakness,' he retorted. 'Our powerpacks are almost exhausted.'

The Doctor turned excitedly back to Scott. 'The androids now know that we can inflict lethal damage on them — so we create a dilemma for them,' he explained.

'But why should they care if we attack the hatch?' Miss Kyle protested wearily.

'They won't *care* — they'll simply *react*,' retorted Nyssa impatiently. 'They have no choice but to obey their programmes.'

The Doctor nodded urgently. 'We create a conflict between duty and survival which should confuse their logic circuits enough to cause them to make mistakes . . .' he concluded triumphantly.

There was an unenthusiastic silence. The Doctor threw Scott a challenging look. 'Well, has anyone a better idea?' he demanded.

The Lieutenant stared hard at the earnest young stranger, a trace of suspicion lingering in his honest eyes, but he knew he had no better plan to offer. 'This had better work,' he muttered at last. He ordered three troopers to aim their laser tubes at the centre of the hatch and the rest of the squad to cover the androids' reaction.

'Now!' he yelled.

With piercing whines the three lasers tore into the metal plate. The two androids tensed, swaying uncertainly from side to side. They seemed unaware of Adric's crouching figure crawling stealthily along a ledge which ran along the tunnel wall behind them. Hesitantly the female android

40

ventured round the buttress and begun to advance. A reckless young trooper stood up from behind the rocks and opened fire, but he was instantly melted by a flash from the male android's surviving hand. At once the advancing female started blasting the squad's positions and the barricade of fallen rock rapidly began to disintegrate around them.

Poising himself on the ledge, Adric picked up a heavy, jagged stone and taking careful aim hurled it with all his strength at the back of the male android's head. It bounced off harmlessly and the creature started to turn round. Quick as lightning, Adric grabbed a larger rock and flung it. The missile struck the side of the android's head as it was about to fire. Adric just had time to throw himself behind the buttress before the tunnel wall cracked and splintered into fragments exactly where he had been standing.

Seizing the chance created by Adric's diversion, the squad concentrated their fire upon the disabled and distracted male, blowing off its head. The female android began to lope towards the hatch as if to protect it with its body, still blasting away at the troopers behind the rockfall. Relentlessly the squad's concentrated laser fire poured into the creature. Its movements grew slower and more staggering. Finally, in a spectacular shower of sparks, it collapsed.

A roar of victory broke the sudden silence. Jumping from the ledge, Adric ventured cautiously into the cavern to find himself being greeted like a conquering hero.

'Well done, Adric, well done!' the Doctor cried, rushing out and almost hugging the confused but smiling boy. 'Not exactly elegant, Adric, but extremely effective. Don't you agree?' he chuckled, turning to Lieutenant Scott.

'Who is that boy?' Scott demanded, filled with admiration.

'This is my good friend, Adric,' the Doctor exclaimed proudly.

In their hushed and darkened lair the two silver figures had watched the destruction of their two androids vividly displayed in the blood-coloured glow of the holovisor disc. Their metal masks betraying nothing, but the sharp snatching sounds from their ventilator units revealed their mounting anger and frustration. They stared down at the blank plate underneath the projector tubes.

'The androids were invaluable. It was an error to sacrifice them,' hissed the larger figure.

'And now the Earthlings are attempting to break through the hatch, Leader,' boomed the other.

'Are their puny weapons capable?'

'It is possible, Leader. They must be stopped.'

The huge Leader loomed over the control module, its eye pods blank but weirdly hypnotic. 'Then we shall be forced to advance our plan. We shall commence activation of the device at once.'

There was a momentary silence.

'But it is much too soon, Leader . . .'

The Leader's massive arm flew up in a dangerous gesture of warning. 'We must be prepared. No more errors will be tolerated. Initiate the carrier signal.'

The subordinate hesitated, sounds of conflict issuing from its inner circuitry as it stared impassively at its superior.

'Initiate the signal!' the Leader repeated in a rasping, hollow voice. 'Now.'

Obediently the subordinate began to operate sequences of switches on the module. Lights flashed. Circuits hummed into life.

'Carrier signal initiated, Leader. Transmission beam locked.'

'Excellent. Activate arming sequence codes.'

Again the smaller figure hesitated. 'It is premature, Leader. The device will be wasted . . .'

'Only time is being wasted,' the Leader boomed. 'Activate the codes.'

Once again the subordinate obeyed, feeding a series of small discs into the module. 'Codes activated, Leader,' it reported eventually.

The Leader emitted a hiss of satisfaction and nodded slowly. 'Excellent. Now the Earth Powers shall witness the superiority of Cyber technology.' It leaned forward, the flashing lights reflected in a bizarre pattern on its immobile face. 'Prepare to detonate the bomb.'

4

A Crisis Defused

The Doctor and Nyssa were kneeling beside the wreckage of the female android, poking about in eager fascination among the lumps of circuitry and silicon tubing.

'Fairly primitive,' Nyssa remarked critically, pulling the head apart with her delicate fingers and peering intently at the remains of the miniature computer.

'You think so?' murmured the Doctor, absorbed in examining the construction of the chest section.

Suddenly Nyssa held up a fused clump of wires. 'Look at this, Doctor!' she exclaimed excitedly.

The Doctor took the component and immediately sprang to his feet, calling Lieutenant Scott over to him. 'I think you should postpone your victory celebrations for the time being,' he told him. 'We must get that hatch open as quickly as possible.'

Scott gestured at the remains of the android. 'Why, Doctor? What's the hurry?'

'One of the androids contained a powerful photosonic transmitter,' Nyssa explained, pointing to the object in the Doctor's hand.

Just then Adric joined them. 'That must have been the cause of the terrible feedback interference I picked up in the TARDIS,' he told them.

The Doctor nodded. 'Very likely. The signals are easy to intercept, but impossible to decode without the proper receiver,' he explained.

Scott looked blankly at them. 'So? What's the problem?'

The Doctor gave a worried frown, 'I'm afraid that

whoever is responsible for that hatch over there now knows that we have destroyed its guardians.' He turned and scrambled over to the rocks towards the hatch. The others followed chattering nervously.

The troopers' lasers had burned an almost circular hole about twenty centimetres in diameter in the centre of the thick metal panel. The Doctor knelt to investigate. Suddenly he whipped his hand away from the hot, blackened edge of the hole. 'Your squad got rather carried away didn't they, Lieutenant?' he complained, sucking his scorched fingers. Then he took out a pen torch and shone it into the darkness, peering as close as he dared. 'I suggest that you stand well clear,' he warned them gravely after a few seconds. 'This might be booby-trapped.'

'What about you?' Scott objected, obviously reluctant to give up his authority.

The Doctor flung out both his arms like aeroplane wings. 'My arms are only this long,' he laughed, 'I can't get any further away.' With that he resumed his examination.

Scott stirred himself. 'Right. Everybody back!' he ordered, shepherding the onlookers across the rocks to safety on the far side of the cavern.

Only Adric was left crouching a little behind the Doctor, who gingerly pushed his arm through the hole and tried to feel about behind the panel. For several minutes the Doctor struggled, attempting to keep his arm away from the molten edge of the hole while manoeuvring his hand inside. 'Got it!' he cried at last. 'The release mechanism.'

Then he noticed Adric. 'I thought I told everyone to get back!' he snapped angrily.

'But Doctor, it's safe. You've checked for booby-traps,' Adric protested.

'I am not in any mood to argue!' the Doctor shouted.

Adric retreated a few paces.

'Further than that,' the Doctor insisted. He waited until Adric had positioned himself behind a large boulder and then he slowly unlocked the mechanism with a series of sharp clicks. Across the cavern, the others craned forward anxiously as the Doctor mopped his brow with his free hand and then gradually started to ease the hatch open. He paused and shone his torch around the few centimetres' gap around the hatchway frame. The space behind the panel was pitch dark and he could just make out vague shapes and bundles of wires in the cramped compartment. Tense and pale, Adric tried to lean round the rock to see better, but he ducked back when the Doctor glanced round to check that everyone was safely under cover.

Deciding that all was safe, the Doctor eased the hatch wide open. There was a blinding bluish flash but no explosion. The Doctor flung himself backwards across the rocks with a startled cry and lay still, momentarily stunned, an eerie blue light pulsing over his shocked features. For a moment no one moved. Then Nyssa, Tegan and Adric rushed to the Doctor's side.

'I thought a booby-trap had gone off . . .' Tegan murmured, helping the Doctor to a sitting position.

'Are you all right, Doctor?' Nyssa asked anxiously.

Adric stared into the pulsating, humming compartment. 'What is it, Doctor?' he exclaimed, frowning at the two large cubes of flickering circuitry connected by a section of fluorescent tubing which was emitting the harsh strobing flashes.

The Doctor struggled onto his knees. 'That is a colossally powerful bomb,' he replied shakily. 'My interference appears to have triggered its arming sequence, I regret to say.' The Doctor shook himself vigorously to clear his dazed head, then he turned to Scott. 'You'd better warn your people on the surface,' he advised him.

46

Scott flicked on his communicator. 'How long have we got?' he demanded.

The Doctor shrugged. 'Perhaps only minutes,' he snapped. He turned urgently to Tegan and Nyssa. 'Get everyone into the TARDIS immediately!' he shouted, crawling painfully back over to the hatchway.

Tegan and Nyssa hesitated for a moment. Then, yelling to the troopers to follow them, they set off hurriedly towards the tunnel.

Adric grabbed the Doctor's shoulder and tried to drag him away. 'Come on, Doctor. You can't stay here,' he insisted.

The Doctor shook himself free. 'It was my own stupidity that set this thing going, Adric,' he retorted, 'and the least I can do is try to stop it.' The Doctor poked frantically about inside the compartment, while Adric looked on in mounting horror.

Scott had been vainly trying to contact Trooper Walters, but his radio produced nothing but a weird oscillating whine. Suddenly the Doctor whipped round and listened for a second or two. Then he thumped himself on the forehead with his fist. 'Of course!' he cried, leaping to his feet and seizing Adric by the arm. 'Come on you two!' and he ran off at breakneck speed towards the TARDIS.

The Cyberleader emitted a vicious, stabbing hiss as a shrill warning siren began to howl from the control module. The Deputy examined the instruments blinking in the gloom.

'The Earthlings have succeeded. They have penetrated the bomb cell, Leader.'

The towering figure waved his arm dismissively. 'The Earthlings are too late. Priming sequence has been initiated?'

'Affirmative, Leader.'

'Then how much longer until detonation?'

'Sixty seconds, Leader. Neutron exchange approaching optimum,' the Deputy reported.

'Excellent,' the Leader replied with a soft, gaseous hiss. He removed a kind of key from his belt and inserted it into a socket on the module. Then with a rasp of satisfaction from his ventilator grille he twisted the key sharply back and forth several times. 'Master detonator released. Proceed to detonation.'

'Affirmative. In fifty-five seconds from now, Leader.'

In its cell deep underground the bomb buzzed and flashed with increasing power in obedience to the signals pulsing across the solar system . . .

'Set all co-ordinates to zero!' the Doctor yelled to Adric who was close on his heels as he rushed into the TARDIS control chamber. Then he ducked under the central console, snatched open a small panel set into the pedestal and rummaged about inside.

'It would be nice to know exactly what you're up to, Doctor,' Adric remarked resentfully as he carried out the Doctor's instructions on the main console.

The Doctor pulled out a tangle of brightly coloured cables, frowned, shook his head and thrust it back again. 'The bomb is being armed by remote control . . .' he explained, pulling out another knot of wires and feverishly trying to untangle them.

'So you could jam it!' Adric suggested eagerly.

'Yes, once I know where its getting its orders from,' the Doctor said, making a few rapid reconnections.

At that moment Scott, Kyle and the troopers entered and stood in awed and astonished silence, staring round the spacious interior of the narrow, shabby old police box.

The Doctor jumped up and flicked a few switches on the console. 'That can't be right!' he frowned. 'Or can it?'

48

'How long does the arming procedure take?' Adric asked nervously while the Doctor dithered about, bobbing up and down from console to pedestal and back again, muttering secretly to himself.

'Not long,' he replied brightly, totally engrossed in his task.

'Well . . . can't I help at all?' Adric demanded. The Doctor did not reply. Adric glanced worriedly at Tegan and Nyssa.

'Shouldn't you move the TARDIS, Doctor?' Tegan asked timidly. 'Before that bomb thing goes off?'

After a few more seconds silence the Doctor jumped up and again checked some instruments on the console. 'We must hurry!' he cried, yanking a kind of drawer brimming with a strange assortment of tools out of the pedestal.

'You've managed to jam the signal?' Nyssa asked hopefully.

'Temporarily. If they increase power they can easily break through again . . .' the Doctor answered, striding to the door. 'Well, come along, Adric. Do try and make yourself useful for a change,' he shouted impatiently and strode outside, leaving the others gaping at each other in uneasy bewilderment while the Doctor's improvised jamming mechanism sparked and throbbed like a heap of multicoloured spaghetti on the console.

Once again the warning siren howled from the Cybermen's control module.

'What is it now?' the Leader demanded, cancelling the warning with a stab of the finger.

'Our control signal is being jammed, Leader,' the Deputy replied after rapidly scanning the array of instruments.

'Jammed?' the Leader boomed menacingly. 'Increase power.'

49

The Deputy obeyed. Immediately the warning sounded again, this time more urgently.

'What is the delay?'

'Overload hazard, Leader. There is resistance from somewhere.'

'Override it at once,' the Leader ordered. 'The primitive technology of the Earthlings cannot resist us.'

The Deputy hesitated. 'But if we drain too much power now . . .'

A savage hiss from the Leader's ventilator unit silenced the Deputy and he hurriedly made the necessary adjustments. 'Supplementary power engaged, Leader.'

'Excellent,' the Leader acknowledged. 'In thirty seconds' time the destruction of Earth will achieve for us the revenge we have sought for so long . . .'

When they returned to the bomb Adric and the Doctor found that it had stopped pulsating and flashing. Swiftly the Doctor set to work to disarm the eerily inert mechanism.

'Magnetic clamp,' he ordered.

Adric rummaged in the tool-box and handed him a device resembling a small pair of square dumb-bells. The Doctor carefully positioned it so that it linked the two cubic components at either end of the glass tube. .

'How much damage could this bomb have done?' Adric asked, handing the Doctor a probe.

'Enough . . .' the Doctor replied enigmatically, poking cautiously about in a mass of small, flexible tubes.

'For what?'

'Enough to blow the entire planet apart if it were sited at the right spot,' the Doctor muttered. 'For example at a focus of geological fault lines . . . Laser cutter, please.'

Adric handed over a compact tool resembling a large fountain pen. 'It's totally bizarre,' he murmured, holding his breath as the Doctor sliced through a thick wire.

'Professor Kyle told me she'd been working down here almost a month before those androids attacked her team. Why did they wait so long?'

'No need to attack until the Professor's investigations brought her too close to their little secret here. Magnetic drone, please.' The Doctor started attaching the small coil Adric passed him to an exposed circuit. Suddenly he jumped back with a yelp of pain and dropped the drone. 'There was power in there,' he said with a puzzled frown, 'and there definitely shouldn't have been.'

At that moment the fluorescent tube began to pulse again intermittently. The Doctor gaped at it in dismay. 'The signal's breaking through again!' he cried as the erratic blue flashes grew quickly stronger and more regular. For a moment the Doctor looked completely defeated. Then he took a deep breath. 'Only one answer — abandon methodical procedure for sheer blind instinct . . .' he declared.

Seizing the laser cutter, the Doctor held it close to the exposed circuit which had given him the shock. He held up crossed fingers on his free hand and smiled at Adric. 'Here we go . . .' he whispered, and he firmly squeezed the trigger.

Inside the TARDIS, Nyssa had been leaning over the console desperately trying to boost the jamming signal being generated by the TARDIS's circuits, while Tegan and the others anxiously watched Adric and the Doctor on the viewer screen. The ominous blue flashes had grown stronger and stronger as the mysterious alien command-signal had increased in power, and Nyssa knew that the Doctor's hastily devised lash-up was approaching its maximum capacity. With sinking heart she realised that the jamming circuit could utilise only a tiny fraction of the TARDIS's enormous energy potential. She glanced in despair at the two puny little figures crouching in front of the hatchway in the pulsating cavern on the viewer. She caught Tegan's eye and slowly shook her head.

'It's stopped . . .' The Professor's joyful cry made them look back at the viewer. The flashing in the cavern had stopped. Nyssa stared down at the console displays.

'It's true,' she cried excitedly. 'They've stopped transmitting. The signal's vanished. The Doctor's done it!'

The Cyberleader strode round and round the control module while the Deputy made rapid adjustments to the holovisor disc mounted on top of it.

'The Earthlings cannot have deactivated the device themselves,' the Leader stormed, 'our technology is too advanced. Either they received help from some superior intelligence, or we have been betrayed. Whoever is responsible will be found and eliminated.'

The Deputy announced that the apparatus was now prepared. Seconds later a replay of the battle between the two androids and the troopers in the cavern began to glow in three-dimension under the projector tubes. The Cybermen watched closely.

'All the alien participants appear to be humans, Leader.'

The Leader raised his arm sharply for silence. On the disc Adric could be seen throwing the second rock at the male android and, just as the android turned to fire at him, the faint image of the TARDIS appeared fleetingly in the background.

'There . . .' the Leader rasped, stabbing a hold button and freezing the image. He then operated an intensifier adjustment and the TARDIS image was magnified and focused in the centre of the disc.

The Leader leaned forward expectantly, his ventilator hissing harshly. 'A TARDIS . . .' he grated.

'Time Lords are forbidden to interfere, Leader,' the Deputy objected.

'This one calls itself "the Doctor",' the Leader boomed, selecting a programme from the holovisor's memory and switching it on again. 'It has assumed a variety of regenerative forms and it does nothing *but* interfere . . .'

On the disc appeared the head of an old man with a narrow face, long hooked nose, flowing white hair and thin lips. He was saying something in an earnest, wavering voice: '. . . but have you no emotions . . . like love, pride, hate, fear . . .?'

The image faded and was succeeded by the head of a dark-skinned man with a fringe of straight black hair, heavy dark eyebrows, brown eyes and a smallish mouth who was leaning forward with a cynical smile which made deep furrows on each side of his nose and saying: '. . . I imagine that you have orders to destroy me . . .'

The Leader jabbed the hold control. 'In this regenerated form, the Doctor confined the Cybermen to their ice tomb on Telos,' he hissed.

The Leader released the control and the glowing image changed once more. This time an enormous head of curly brown hair appeared, a huge face with staring blue eyes and a wide mouth curling with contempt. The image loomed over the disc as a deep, rich voice ranted mockingly: 'You're just a pathetic bunch of tin soldiers scuttling about the galaxy in an ancient spaceship . . .'

The holovisor went dark.

'It was in that last regeneration that the Doctor defeated our attempts to destroy Voga,' the Leader concluded.

At the mention of the planet Voga the Deputy had clasped both hands protectively across his ventilator grille. 'The planet of *gold* . . .' he hissed convulsively. For a few seconds both Cybermen uttered a curious gasping and choking sound before recovering their composure.

'Leader,' the Deputy objected eventually, 'none of those creatures appears in the cavern with the Earthlings.'

'The reason for that is obvious,' the Leader declared. 'Our enemy, the Doctor, has regenerated once again . . .'

On his triumphant return to the TARDIS, the Doctor modestly brushed aside the barrage of congratulations awaiting him and immediately concentrated on dismantling the lash-up still littering the console and on preparations for departure. Scott and the Professor tried hard to persuade him to remain on Earth just a little longer.

'But you have done so much, Doctor. We want to express our gratitude,' pleaded Professor Kyle.

'Thank you, but we must leave,' the Doctor insisted. 'There is still a great deal to do.'

'Haven't you done quite enough for one day, Doctor?' Tegan teased him, though she was feeling fairly shaken underneath.

Adric threatened to grow argumentative. 'We could surely spare a few hours, Doctor?' he objected.

But the Doctor shook his head firmly and busied himself with adjusting the navigational instruments. 'There just isn't time,' he told them.

'So. Where are we hurrying off to now?' Nyssa demanded with a challenging air, as if to catch the Doctor out.

'Sector Sixteen.'

'Oh beaut! Sounds great fun!' Tegan scoffed.

'The Doctor is anxious to meet the creators of the androids,' Adric announced.

'So you know who they are!' Scott exclaimed in surprise.

The Doctor looked up sharply. 'No. I only know where their transmissions originated.'

The Lieutenant gestured to Professor Kyle and the handful of surviving troopers. 'Then you must take us with you, Doctor.'

The Doctor shook his head emphatically and fussed over the console.

'Well, we can't fight androids all by ourselves, Doctor,' Nyssa pointed out acidly.

'I hope that will not be necessary, Nyssa,' the Doctor retorted. He straightened up and turned to the Lieutenant. 'I'm afraid I shall have to ask you and your friends to leave now,' he said politely.

Scott planted himself firmly in front of the Doctor and folded his arms. 'Look here, if our planet's being threatened we insist on doing everything we can to defend it,' he snapped.

The Doctor opened his mouth as if to deliver an ultimatum and promptly shut it again. He glanced round at the determined faces assembled before him. 'All right,' he said leaning across and flicking the exterior door lever, 'but you'd better hold on tight. We'll be away in no time at all . . .'

The newcomers stared at each other with a mixture of amusement and amazement as the TARDIS shuddered violently and started to make a noise like a cross between trumpeting elephants and tearing metal. The floor bucked and reared like an unbroken steer, before steadying into a gentle swinging motion.

'Please make yourselves at home,' the Doctor urged reassuringly. 'Nyssa and Tegan will show you where everything is.'

As the strangers were being ushered out, the Doctor buttonholed Adric. 'Do you have a moment?' he asked with a smile.

'Well, I am rather hungry,' Adric mumbled, reluctantly closing the internal door.

The Doctor cleared his throat awkwardly, thrust his hands deep into his pockets and paced up and down uncomfortably. 'Adric, I'm . . . I'm very grateful for all your help . . . with the bomb and with that android . . .' he muttered almost inaudibly.

'That's quite all right. All in a day's work,' Adric shrugged.

The Doctor stopped in front of him. 'Look . . . I've been thinking about your wish to return home . . .' he began.

'And?'

'And . . . well if we could work out a satisfactory course I just might . . . I just might . . . well, give it a try.'

'Oh I've already done that,' Adric said off-handedly. 'It's there on the pad.'

The Doctor looked very disconcerted. 'Really?' he laughed, picking up the pad from the console and flicking through it, his eyebrows rising higher and higher as he did so.

'As you'll see I've managed to compute the position of the CVE . . .'

'Oh you've done remarkably well,' the Doctor said admiringly.

'Thank you,' Adric replied politely, opening the door.

The Doctor fluttered the pages of the notepad again. 'Look Adric, I'm really sorry about our little disagreement earlier on,' he managed to mumble, blushing with embarrassment.

'I over-reacted,' Adric said graciously.

'Do you really want to go home?'

Adric grinned broadly. 'No, of course not, Doctor. There's nothing for me there now,' he admitted.

'You mean you did all this work for nothing?' the Doctor cried incredulously, waving the notebook.

'It made my point,' Adric replied. 'And who knows — I might change my mind. Again!'

5

Stowaways

Not far beyond the orbit of the remotest planet in the solar
system a gigantic bulk freighter of the Galactic Services
Commission hung motionless in space. Its colossal hulk
dwarfed the small, elegant, wheel-shaped space-station
revolving slowly on its axis near by. The freighter
resembled an irregular cluster of vast steel buildings with
other smaller ones added on all over it as a kind of
afterthought. Its hundreds of exterior surfaces bristled with
antennae and revolving dishes and hatches of all shapes and
sizes. In stark contrast to the brilliantly illuminated port-
holes of the space-station, the freighter loomed dark and
unwelcoming. One tiny section, high up at one end,
displayed a few faint lights through the observation ports of
the navigation bridge.

Inside, the bridge was long, wide and low-ceilinged and
almost every available surface was crammed with displays,
instruments and controls. At one end was a long low console with banks of screens suspended above, and two large
heavily-padded seats with high backs positioned on a low
dais in front of it. At the other end of the bridge were two
sets of sliding doors leading into the main body of the ship,
and in between, set into the side of the bridge, was an
emergency airlock with ESCAPE POD stencilled in red. Most
of the floor space was occupied by cabinets containing
computers and navigational devices. The air was warm and
filled with low humming and electronic chattering sounds.

In one of the command seats a lean hard woman of about
fifty with straight fair hair and a boney pear-shaped face

was sitting reading. She was wearing a faded greyish uniform, quite plain except for First Officer flashes on the shoulders. Near by, a tall sinewy young man with chiselled features and very short dark hair was standing stiffly upright, staring blankly at the image of the space-station on one of the monitor screens. He wore a similar uniform but with Navigator flashes. His thin hands were clasping and unclasping nervously behind his back.

'The Captain's been gone for hours,' he said in a thin nasal voice.

The woman turned a page of her book. 'Everything will be all right, Ringway,' she replied complacently after a pause.

The young man gave a hollow laugh. 'I wish I had your confidence, Berger. Three crewmen disappear without trace in the last two weeks: a word in the wrong place and we could be stuck out here for weeks, pending an inquiry.'

'No one's going to breathe a word,' Berger said soothingly without raising her eyes. 'They all know that any delay now will cost them their bonuses.'

Ringway narrowed his eyes at the screen as if he were trying to see into the interior of the space-station. 'Don't be too sure,' he snapped, 'morale is very low.'

Berger turned another page. 'Well, yours obviously is,' she laughed. 'But you're supposed to be an officer, Ringway. Try smiling to the crew occasionally. Reassure them.'

The young Navigator spun round angrily, but before he could speak, a voice announced over the ship's intercom that the Captain had just come aboard.

First Officer Berger snapped her book shut and stood up. 'There. Mum's home again,' she scoffed. 'How's that for morale?'

One of the access doors zipped smartly aside and a short but fierce-looking woman with elegantly styled coppery hair and a pale sharp face walked wearily onto the bridge. She was about the same age as Berger, but her green eyes were piercingly alert. She was wearing a black jerkin with a high wide collar, grey trousers tucked into black boots and black gloves.

'Take that straight to my cabin,' she ordered in a brittle, haughty voice as two crewmen carrying a heavy metal trunk followed her in.

Ringway stood sharply to attention. 'Welcome aboard, Ma'am,' he said crisply.

'Don't call me Ma'am on the bridge,' the Captain snapped, thrusting a cassette transponder into Ringway's hands as she brushed past him, 'and get that plugged into the computer immediately. I want to get under way.' She glanced briefly at the console displays and then dropped heavily into her command seat and shut her eyes. 'Seven hours . . . seven hours they kept me hanging about. I'm exhausted,' she complained.

First Officer Berger glanced across at Ringway, but he appeared to be engrossed in installing the transponder. 'Problems with Security?' she asked casually.

'Not really. It's just that Earth's on red alert,' the Captain replied sarcastically. 'There's some Galactic Congress being held, so they're being a bit fussier than usual. We won't have any more trouble. I've got a priority clearance straight through to Earth.' She opened her eyes and hauled herself to her feet. 'Our bonus is safe,' she said with a glacial smile.

'So there wasn't any mention of the missing crew members?' Ringway asked anxiously.

'Panicking again, were we, Mister Ringway?' the Captain laughed, swaggering across the bridge. 'Well, you can relax. Nothing was said.'

'I just happen to consider the unexplained disappearance of three crew members rather important, Captain,' Ringway muttered through clenched teeth.

59

'Oh so do I, Ringway, so do I . . .' the Captain retorted sharply. 'But it will be investigated after we've reached Earth and safely discharged our cargo. Understood?'

'Yes, Captain Briggs,' the Navigator replied submissively.

'If it will make you any happier, you can increase the patrols,' Briggs added contemptuously. 'But I don't want to hear any more about the business. You are beginning to bore me.'

A few minutes later, departure preparations had been completed and Captain Briggs took a final look round the bridge. 'I'm glad you're on first watch,' she said to Berger. 'Good luck. I'm off to freshen myself up.'

Ringway had crossed to a panel in the wall and was inserting his thumb into the identification lock. 'Just thought I ought to check the security patrols,' he explained in response to Briggs's enquiring stare, 'especially with so many of the surveillance cameras on the blink at the moment.'

'But I need you up here!' Berger protested, working busily at the main console.

Briggs frowned at the bank of small security monitors, only about half of which were functioning properly. 'Oh let him check the patrols, it'll be good for morale. Don't get lost!' she cried, marching out with a whooping laugh.

Ringway's small eyes watched Berger sitting with her back to him as she coolly and efficiently got the freighter under way. He opened the armoury compartment and took out a laser pistol. 'Why does Briggs always run me down?' he asked bitterly, clipping the pistol onto his belt.

'Perhaps you shouldn't sound quite so earnest all the time,' Berger replied without looking round.

Ringway stood frowning at the security monitors for a moment. Then he closed the armoury panel and went out through the access door leading to the main hold, a cynical smile creeping gradually over his pinched features.

The freighter's main hold was a vast echoing structure, hundreds of metres in length and width, and tens of metres high. A series of catwalks criss-crossed it, joining several tiers of walkways running around the walls and leading down at regular intervals to the vast floor via open metal stairways. Soft fluorescent lighting cast an eerie twilight from the lofty ceiling. The hold was filled with hundreds of tall silos, each shaped like a cluster of broad cylinders standing on end in a rectangular formation. The silos were arranged in rows, and the rows in groups, so that long narrow corridors ran at right angles between them down the length and breadth of the hold. These long deep corridors between the silos were full of gigantic shadows and dark corners. Occasionally, faint shudders reverberated through the huge space as if some species of monstrous animal were stirring quietly somewhere in the depths . . .

All at once a muffled grinding and scraping noise erupted down in a far corner of the after end of the hold. The TARDIS blinked uncertainly into tangible form and fell silent.

Inside, everyone was staring expectantly at the viewer.

'Well, here we are!' the Doctor announced reassuringly, smiling broadly at the dazed expressions on the faces of the Lieutenant, Professor Kyle and the troopers.

'Where's here?' Tegan demanded suspiciously.

Nyssa checked the console. 'The atmosphere is breathable,' she reported.

The Doctor shrugged. 'It looks like the interior of some kind of cargo vessel,' he said, nodding at the unfriendly shadows on the screen. 'But appearances can be deceptive, of course.'

61

Pulling himself together, Scott turned to his squad. 'We should move in before anyone realises we're here,' he said.

The Doctor stared disapprovingly at the Lieutenant's laser tube. 'That way innocent people might get hurt,' he scolded.

Scott laughed. 'Doesn't worry me, Doctor. These people tried to destroy my planet,' he retorted.

The Doctor smiled patiently. 'We don't know that for certain.'

'But this is where the beam controlling the bomb originated?' Kyle interrupted.

The Doctor raised his hands in a calming gesture. 'My experience through several hundred years has taught me not to jump to hasty conclusions,' he said quietly.

The Lieutenant suddenly looked extremely travel-sick. The full realisation of what had just happened to him and to his squad inside the Doctor's museum piece seemed to overwhelm him. He nodded meekly. 'Of course, Doctor . . . whatever you think best . . . several hundred years . . .' he mumbled queasily, trying unsuccessfully to hide his confusion.

'Good. Then we'll start with a small recce,' the Doctor announced, opening the exterior door and putting on his hat.

Adric sprang forward. 'I'm coming with you.'

The Doctor paused. For a split second it seemed that he was going to refuse and Adric prepared for battle. 'Certainly Adric,' the Doctor cried and he peered cautiously round the door.

'Which way?' Adric whispered.

The Doctor stepped outside and glanced around. 'I don't think it very much matters,' he cried, thrusting his hands into his pockets and setting briskly off into the shadows.

Scott watched them on the viewer. 'I should have gone with them,' he muttered, appalled by the Doctor's jaunty air as he strode swiftly out of vision.

Just then a throaty klaxon noise sounded from the console.

'What's that?' Scott demanded jumpily.

Nyssa frowned and fiddled with some buttons. 'That *is* interesting . . .' she exclaimed in surprise. 'This freighter or whatever it is has just accelerated into warp drive!'

On the holovisor disc the TARDIS was materialising all over again deep among the silos. The Cyberleader watched intently the image glowing beneath the projector tubes as the door opened and the figures of the Doctor and Adric came out.

'Excellent . . . Excellent . . .' he hissed, leaning forward.

'It seems that your revenge will come sooner than expected, Leader,' rasped the Deputy, adjusting the projectors.

'Indeed,' boomed the Leader. 'Our contingency plan can now proceed. The destruction of Earth is assured.'

A harsh bleeping tone sounded from the module. The Leader stabbed a button on the communications panel. 'Report.'

'The freighter has received full security clearance for Earth, Leader,' said a thin nasal voice distorted in the speaker.

'Excellent.'

'But there is a problem. The disappearance of the three crewmembers is causing unrest . . .'

The Cyberleader's blank eye-pods were riveted on the ghostly image of the Doctor and Adric walking away from the TARDIS. 'Instruct your minions to search the hold,' he ordered. 'You will find a scapegoat there.'

There was a buzzing pause. 'Leader?' the voice queried hesitantly.

'You have intruders,' the Cyberleader boomed, and he

jabbed the communicator off, signing to the Deputy to replay the materialisation of the TARDIS yet again.

Two young crewmen — Vance and Buchanan — were patrolling slowly along the first-level walkway above the main hold, their laser tubes slung over their shoulders, grumbling about their duties and about life on the freighter in general.

'I don't fancy walking round that lot,' Vance muttered, glancing down at the endless rows of silos stretching like a miniature town below them. 'Ringway should do his own patrols.'

'You could hide an army down there and never find it,' joked Buchanan as they reached a metal stairway and started to descend.

Half-way down, Vance suddenly stopped. 'What's that?' he whispered, whipping his laser off his shoulder.

'Where?'

'I saw something move. By silo 529.'

'Nothing there now,' Buchanan shrugged. 'Anyway it's pitch dark.'

'Better look, though,' Vance insisted.

'I suppose so,' Buchanan agreed grudgingly. 'You and your carrot juice!'

Reluctantly they crept down to the main floor and began edging along the dark narrow corridor between two rows of towering silos.

Up on the walkway, at the bridge end of the hold, Navigating Officer Ringway stood in the shadows carefully retuning the frequency on his communicator. 'Ringway to Vance. Report position, please,' he murmured into it in his nasal whine.

'Vance here, sir. Just passing silo 519 at floor level. We've spotted someone.'

A thin smile just cracked the corners of Ringway's

emaciated face. 'Then apprehend him. I'll be right down,' he snapped, unclipping his pistol and hurrying towards a nearby stairway.

Vance and his mate had pressed themselves into the shallow niche formed by the curving sides of silo 529 and were watching a large obscure shadow moving from niche to niche further along the row of silos. Suddenly it disappeared completely.

'This way. We'll head him off,' Vance muttered excitedly. He darted across the junction where two corridors crossed at right angles. 'I think we've got him now.'

They ran along one side of a block of silos, turned and then crept rapidly along the other side to the next junction, where they waited in ambush. They waited in vain.

'Lost him again,' Vance spat.

As he spoke, Buchanan gripped his arm and pointed back the way they had just come. They just caught a glimpse of a tall glinting figure crossing along one of the transverse corridors some distance away. They stared at one another in astonishment.

Vance rubbed his eyes. 'How did he get over there so fast?' he exclaimed.

'Perhaps there's more than one of them,' Buchanan murmured, priming his laser, 'whatever it is.'

'I don't like this,' Vance said, checking his own weapon. 'Come on . . .' he breathed, setting off back the way they had come.

Buchanan tapped on a silo wall with his knuckles before moving warily after Vance. 'What's in these things anyway?' he whispered uneasily . . .

'Aren't we being just a little bit casual?' Adric suggested, struggling to keep up as the Doctor breezed along between the silos, turning left or right at whim.

'Oh there's no one about. This ship is totally automated,' retorted the Doctor airily.

'There must be some kind of crew.'

'Perhaps a small one. Somewhere.' The Doctor had stopped abruptly in front of a small security camera angled along the alleyway and was bowing and doffing his hat at the lens in exaggerated politeness.

Adric shook his head resignedly. 'I don't like being so far away from the TARDIS,' he complained. 'Could we go back now?'

'Give them a chance!' the Doctor protested, smiling and waving at the camera. 'I want to announce my presence.'

Adric tapped the metal side of the nearest silo, marked 533, and put his ear up against it. 'Sounds empty,' he muttered.

'Come along!' cried the Doctor, setting off again. As they hurried along, a tall shadow followed them, flapping and whipping over the curved walls of the silos.

Adric started glancing uneasily over his shoulder. 'Doctor, I've suddenly got the feeling we were spotted a long time ago . . .' he breathed.

The Doctor rubbed his hands approvingly and quickened his step. 'You mean we're being followed?' he whispered loudly with a grin.

'Why don't they show themselves?' Adric demanded unhappily.

Suddenly they both froze as two prolonged and piercing screams tore through the hold. The horrifying sound lingered, echoing round the dark recesses between the silos for several seconds.

Adric spun round and stared back down the alleyway. There was nothing there.

The Doctor had turned pale. 'This way,' he whispered and ran swiftly off along a side corridor with Adric hard on his heels. The hold was filled with a raucous klaxon alarm which made the hair rise on the backs of their necks. In a few seconds, they stumbled across the bodies of Vance and Buchanan sprawled in the shadows. They had been savagely beaten to death.

'What a mess,' Adric gasped, wincing at the fearful wounds gouged in the crewmen's heads. 'Doctor, let's get out of here before we're caught and blamed.'

The Doctor knelt beside the bodies rapt in thought. 'They're dead. I've seen injuries inflicted this way before . . .' he mused, as if trying hard to remember something.

Adric seized his shoulder. 'This is hardly the time for a trip down memory lane, Doctor,' he protested nervously.

The Doctor leant over and gently closed the corpses' wildly staring eyes. Then he stood up. 'Coming, Adric . . .' he murmured quietly.

They turned to find themselves up against the barrel of Ringway's laser pistol. His bloodless lips were pressed tightly together and his grey eyes smouldered with anger. 'Stowaways!' he breathed. The pistol emitted a faint whirring sound as Ringway aimed it into their faces. 'On this ship we execute murderers!' he whined.

'Then I sincerely hope that you make sure that you execute the right people,' the Doctor retorted. He gestured at the two brutally beaten victims. 'How could we have done this without covering ourselves in blood?' he demanded logically.

Ringway said nothing.

'And we are not stowaways. We have transport of our own,' Adric added feebly, gesturing vaguely across the hold.

'No tricks!' Ringway snapped. 'Stowaways or pirates — you're still murderers. Now move!' He jerked his head in the direction of the nearest stairway leading up to bridge level. The prisoners reluctantly began walking with Ringway covering them from behind.

Suddenly the Doctor stopped and turned sharply. 'How do you know they are dead?' he said challengingly.

Ringway's finger twitched slightly and his pistol emitted another short burst of whirring. 'Don't tempt me . . .' he said harshly, forcing them forward again.

When they had gone, a huge black shadow suddenly stretched across the two bleeding corpses. As it lingered a moment the air was filled with a rhythmic hissing. Then, with a flash of silver, the mysterious figure disappeared.

6

Monstrous Awakenings

The Cyberleader had watched the capture of Adric and the Doctor with fascinated concentration as it was revealed in vivid detail on the holovisor disc.

'Even under threat of death the Doctor displays all the arrogance characteristic of a Time Lord,' he exclaimed, leaning forward, the faint mechanical and electronic sounds beginning to speed up inside him. 'The Doctor must remain alive so that he can suffer for all our past humiliations . . .' he concluded with chilling deliberation.

'It is time to secure the freighter,' the Deputy announced, moving round the module to the main panel and waiting expectantly for instructions.

The Cyberleader switched off the holovisor as Adric and the Doctor were marched away. 'It is time. Activate the first taskforce,' he ordered. 'The crew is small. They will offer little resistance.'

The Deputy keyed a series of commands into the module. 'Condensors maximum charge, Leader.'

'Excellent. Stabilise and activate.'

The Deputy gave a master key a half-turn. A faint, subterranean grinding noise suddenly rumbled through the freighter. The Deputy turned sharply. 'The commander of the freighter will know that his electrical reserves are being tapped,' he warned.

The Leader rasped menacingly. 'Why did you not jam their instruments?' he demanded.

The Deputy hesitated, staring blankly at the instruments clustered on the module. 'Our drain on the supply is excessive, Leader. The freighter's computers will be alerted.'

Inside the Cyberleader the circuits flashed faster and faster with increasing precision. 'Then we shall take the bridge at once,' he ordered. 'Accelerate reactivation to optimum immediately. This time there must be no failure.'

Again the Deputy hesitated. A low, angry buzzing sound suddenly began to issue from the Cyberleader's enormous silver head. Slowly and reluctantly the Deputy completed the full turn of the master key . . .

Not far away, in another silo, huge cocoon-like objects were ranged motionless in the darkness. Beneath manifold layers of transparent plastic wrapping, enormous silver forms stood erect and silent. In the vast tomb-like space the creatures waited. They were not living, they were not dead. They were waiting to be born.

At last there began a faint crackle, as if a chrysalis were starting to split open and release the imprisoned glory of some beautiful butterfly. Something flickered and tore through the protective layers: first a powerful, stubby finger and then a ripping, shredding hand. Then an arm jerked spasmodically and with a vicious slicing movement carved the plastic shroud asunder.

Laboured gurgling sounds gradually settled into a rhythmic hissing breathing and eerie electronic clicks developed into a relentlessly logical chattering. The silo echoed with the savage infant movements as the Cybermen burst out of the chrysalids and took their first uncertain steps.

Subdued shudders rippled through the freighter, almost as if it knew it was giving birth to the silver horror concealed in its bowels . . .

'Reaction levels normal, Leader,' the Deputy reported in a

strangely hushed tone, the module instruments reflecting in a sinister pattern on his metallic face.

'Excellent. Prepare to engage autonomous control mode.' The Cyberleader watched as the Deputy slowly moved a sliding switch, his ventilator emitting a constant hiss of anticipation.

'Mode engaging in five seconds . . .' the Deputy affirmed.

The enormous fingers on the Cyberleader's hands twitched slightly as they hovered over the module. 'So,' he hissed, 'my army awakes.'

Captain Briggs had returned to the bridge in a foul temper after being disturbed. She slouched in her command seat, yawning and rubbing her eyes and wincing at the screech of the security alert.

'Turn that damn thing off,' she snapped at Berger, who was working away at the bank of surveillance monitors, trying to get them all operational again. Briggs waited impatiently for the prisoners to be brought in, drumming on the arm of her seat and struggling with the jammed zipper of her jerkin.

A few minutes later Ringway marched in with Adric and the Doctor at gunpoint. 'These two were apprehended by silo 550 Captain,' he reported smugly.

Briggs clicked her tongue and cast her eyes towards the ceiling. ' "Apprehended" . . . why don't you say "caught"? You're so melodramatic,' she complained.

Ringway told her about the murdered crew members.

Briggs jumped up and stamped furiously up and down. 'That's all we need!' she cried exasperatedly.

The Doctor took off his hat politely. 'I do assure you, Madam, that you have the wrong people,' he said calmly.

'Quiet!' Ringway snarled, waving his pistol.

Captain Briggs turned on him sharply. 'Thank you, Mister Ringway but I can fight my own battles,' she said with withering scorn. 'You'll get your extra bonus.'

'Thank you, Captain, but I'd rather have Vance and Buchanan alive,' Ringway retorted in an accusing tone.

For a moment Briggs looked as though she would fling herself at Ringway, but she controlled herself and turned to the Doctor with a sour smile. 'And I suppose you're going to tell me that you know nothing about my three missing crew either.'

'How could we? We've only just arrived on board your ship, Madam,' replied the Doctor courteously.

Briggs gave a strange, whooping laugh. 'Only just arrived . . .' she echoed, as if enjoying a joke. Then her face hardened. 'Well someone is responsible . . .' she snarled.

'It isn't us,' Adric protested aggressively.

At that moment a warning tone sounded from the main console and a computer print-out started chattering furiously.

'Another power surge, Captain,' First Officer Berger cried, turning apprehensively to the monitors displaying elaborate coloured diagrams of the freighter's systems. 'But the tracer circuits are still completely jammed.'

'Not again!' Briggs moaned, clasping her head in both hands.

A faint tremor vibrated through the ship and the Doctor instinctively stepped forward to examine the monitors.

'Is this your doing?' Briggs demanded, her mouth drawn tight with suspicion. Ringway's laser whirred softly.

Ignoring Ringway and his threatening attitude, the Doctor turned earnestly to the Captain. 'We may not have much time . . .' he warned her. As quickly and simply as he could, he explained the events which had brought them to the freighter. Briggs and Berger listened with increasing incredulity while Ringway watched the Doctor with a dangerous frown.

When the Doctor had finished, Briggs gaped at him for several seconds in silence, her angular features flushed and

72

blotchy. 'A bomb . . . on Earth . . . controlled from this ship!' she scoffed at last. 'Are you a comedy troupe or something?'

'At least the story's original,' Berger muttered, desperately trying to make some sense of the mysterious readings on the instruments.

'Every word of it is true!' Adric insisted indignantly.

Captain Briggs thrust her face close to the Doctor's. 'Are you trying to make a fool of me?' she murmured menacingly.

Ringway flourished his pistol impatiently. 'He's obviously just playing for time,' he sneered.

The Doctor spoke confidentially to the Captain. 'You have admitted yourself that things have happened which you cannot explain,' he reminded her reasonably.

'It doesn't follow that there's a gang of conspirators hidden aboard my ship planning to blow up the Earth!' she shouted shrilly, pacing agitatedly in front of the console.

'Your crew members who disappeared or were murdered may have discovered otherwise . . .' the Doctor said quietly, with a penetrating stare at Ringway.

Ringway snorted. 'All this is just a diversion, Captain.'

Once again the systems warning sounded urgently from the console.

'It's happening again,' Berger cried distractedly. This time she succeeded in instructing the computer to search for the source of the power loss.

The Doctor watched carefully as a fluorescent tracer blip began rushing along the enormously complex grid showing the ship's electrical systems on the display monitor. 'How often has this occurred?' he asked.

'Several times since we left Toobes Major, but never on this scale before,' Berger replied. Just then the blip stopped and a whole section of the electronic diagram started flashing. 'The main hold!' Berger exclaimed in astonishment.

The Captain spun round abruptly. 'Mister Ringway take a squad down there immediately,' she ordered.

The Navigating Officer hesitated, glancing from Briggs to the Doctor and back again.

'What are you carrying in those silos?' the Doctor asked, frowning at the spasmodic flickering of the few surveillance monitors still operating.

'Mineral ores,' Ringway blurted out, a merest hint of bravado passing over his pinched features as the laser pistol wavered slightly in his clammy grasp.

Briggs slapped her gloved hand against the back of her seat with sudden impatient savagery, glaring at Ringway. At once he pulled himself together and strode obediently out.

'You must isolate the affected section,' the Doctor advised.

'Not while we're in warp drive,' Briggs snapped.

'It's the only way you'll stop them.'

Torn between suspicion and helplessness, the Captain turned in frustration to the Doctor. 'But who are they?' she demanded.

The Doctor shrugged. 'I don't know yet, but I suspect that whatever is tapping your power circuits wants a lot more than just control of your ship.'

Berger jumped up in alarm as more warnings flashed on the console in front of her. 'Captain, we must come out of warp drive now,' she pleaded. 'If we continue to lose power like this the thrusters could mis-phase.'

'No!' Briggs shouted, with a ferocity that surprised everyone. 'I am not risking my bonus just because of a few miserable stowaways.' She walked contemptuously away.

'You must listen,' the Doctor insisted, rushing over and seizing her by the shoulders. 'The story about the bomb is true. Whoever planted it is now concealed in your hold.'

Briggs shook her head vehemently. 'I will not stop this ship,' she bellowed. 'Our transponder would inform Earth Security that we had deviated from our flight schedule. We would be intercepted and hove to. I'd be penalised for delayed delivery.'

'Are you sure you know what you're delivering?' the Doctor challenged her, a gleam of victory in his eyes. 'You could be giving the enemies of Earth a guaranteed free ride.'

Briggs shoved the Doctor aside and dropped heavily into her command seat. 'Ringway,' she snapped into the inter-com, keeping her eyes closely on the Doctor, 'position your squad along the first level. Make sure that whatever's down there stays there.'

'Yes, Captain,' Ringway answered smartly.

'I have no reason to believe your fairy tales,' Briggs told the Doctor.

The Doctor had completely crushed his hat between his hands in his anxiety. He glanced helplessly at Adric and at Berger for support. 'Then at least believe your own instruments!' he finally yelled in exasperation.

Briggs leaned intently over her command panel. 'We go on . . .' she said firmly.

Ever since the departure of the Doctor and Adric, the atmosphere in the TARDIS had grown steadily more tense. In the oppressive silence, Tegan and Professor Kyle were gazing apprehensively at the vague shadowy images on the viewer screen. Scott was pacing around like a caged animal, and the troopers were hanging restlessly about, desperate to get to grips with the enemy — whatever it might be. Nyssa had been fiddling at the console for some time, biting her lip and frowning at strange readings on the instrument panels.

Eventually Scott could contain himself no longer. 'I

think we've waited long enough,' he said, checking his watch.

'I agree. Something must have happened to them,' the Professor murmured.

Nyssa looked up sharply. 'My instinct is to wait,' she objected.

'Why? They've been gone ages,' Tegan protested.

'I'm as concerned as you are,' Nyssa replied, 'but things do not feel right out there.'

'Is the magnetic field still increasing?' Kyle asked.

Nyssa shook her head. 'It's reducing now, but it's still massive.'

They all stared at the mysterious shadows on the viewer.

'Could it hurt them?' Tegan asked quietly.

Nyssa looked very worried. 'I can't tell without knowing what is causing it,' she said. 'We shall just have to wait until it stabilises.'

Reluctantly they waited. Time dragged by and still the screen showed nothing but deep, jagged shadows. At last even Nyssa could bear it no longer. 'The field is much weaker now. It might be safe now . . .' she said uncertainly.

Immediately Scott and his squad snatched up their equipment and stood poised for action, while Nyssa completed a final check.

'I want to come with you!' Tegan suddenly blurted out, grasping the Lieutenant's arm.

Scott shook his head firmly. 'It's going to be very rough, young lady,' he told her rather patronisingly.

Tegan's chin promptly jutted defiantly forward. 'I think I'd find it rougher waiting around in here,' she retorted. She swung round on a startled Professor Kyle. 'Lend me your overalls, Professor,' she ordered cheekily.

'But you're not trained for combat . . .' Scott started to protest.

'Knowing my friends are in danger is all the training I

need!' Tegan snapped, grabbing the Professor's arm and leading her towards an interior door.

Nyssa looked up from her calculations. 'I shouldn't bother to argue, Lieutenant,' she advised as the door closed behind them.

While Tegan and Professor Kyle were changing, Scott took one of the troopers' radios and placed it on the console. 'If the Doctor returns, call me at once,' he told Nyssa. 'I don't want to be out there any longer than necessary.'

A moment later, the interior door flew open and Tegan strode in wearing Professor Kyle's rather too-large overalls and boots. Despite the tense atmosphere, Nyssa found herself suppressing a strong urge to shriek with laughter. Scott just stared open-mouthed as Tegan picked up a spare laser tube dropped by a dead trooper in the cavern earlier.

'Right,' Tegan cried, striding to the exterior door. 'Let's march . . .'

Ringway and his small squad of crew members had hastily constructed a rough barricade of crates and drums around the top of the steel stairway leading down from the bridge level to the floor of the main hold. While they worked, they kept glancing down into the silent shadowy labyrinth below the walkway, but so far nothing had stirred among the dark cold canyons between the massive silos.

Then all at once, a noise like the savage screeching of some gigantic primitive bird ripped through the ominous stillness. The crew froze as the sound of violently tearing and twisting metal reached an echoing climax and then abruptly ceased.

'To your positions,' Ringway hissed. The terrified squad scrambled for cover and waited, their lasers whirring in their trembling hands.

For a moment there was silence. Then a dull, rhythmic

beating sound began far down the length of the vast hold. It was accompanied by a low hissing, like the distant breathing of some monstrous animal. The sounds grew relentlessly nearer and nearer, and became more like the working of a vast bellows or some ancient steam engine. One or two of the squad glanced round as if seeking instructions from Ringway — but he was nowhere to be seen.

The crew members stared open-mouthed as a phalanx of silver figures suddenly came into view from the far end of the hold, marching inexorably towards them like a machine. In the midst of the group towered the Cyberleader, its huge head glinting in the shafts of light between the silos. Each Cyberman held its weapon levelled like a stubby cluster of short tubes . . .

Eventually one of the crew members fired his laser. The lethal, pencil-thin beam of energy shot down the corridor between the silos and into the advancing enemy. A few sparks crackled off the armoured silver carapaces. Otherwise the laser had no effect. In sudden panic, all the crew members fired at the strange, robotic creatures. Showers of sparks flew all round the Cybermen, but still they approached unharmed, their empty eyes fixed hypnotically on the barricade above them. The air was filled with the repeated whining of the useless lasers and the spectacular blaze of sparks.

When the Cybermen reached the bottom of the stairway, a fusillade of sickening, invisible bursts thudded out of the ends of their blunt-nosed weapons. Beseiged crew members and bits of barricade were hurled in all directions like leaves in a sudden gust of wind. Still firing their lasers, the surviving defenders desperately tried to retreat towards the bridge as the Cybermen began to climb slowly up the stairway. Burst after burst from the attackers sent more and more of them reeling, their bodies pulped by ultrasonic waves.

When the Cybermen reached the remains of the barricade, they simply marched through it, trampling the heavy steel drums and crates like matchwood . . .

Scott, Tegan and the troopers had been creeping cautiously among the silos, searching anxiously for the Doctor and Adric and trying to locate the source of the weird and terrifying sounds that had begun almost as soon as they had left the TARDIS.

'We'll never find them here,' Tegan complained, tired and frightened.

'You insisted on coming,' Scott reminded her brusquely.

Tegan peered fearfully into the shadows. 'I know,' she sighed, 'I'm just a mouth on legs really. I just wish I could keep it shut occasionally . . .' She fell abruptly silent, but her mouth still hung wide open. Speechless, she pointed down a corridor at right angles to the one they had been following. There hung the remains of a silo that seemed as if it had exploded: the thick metal walls were split and peeled back like torn paper.

They stared at the fearsome wreckage a moment, then Scott led them slowly closer, lasers primed. The huge container was empty except for a mass of shredded plastic sheeting scattered like twisted broken cobweb over the floor.

Just then, a series of sickening thuds throbbed through the hold followed by the clatter of flying metal and horrifying human screams.

'The Doctor?' Scott gasped, turning to a chalk-white Tegan. 'Follow me!' he whispered, leading them swiftly through the silos towards the noise.

By the time they reached the end of the hold near the bridge stairway, the firing had stopped. Crouching in the deep shadows, they watched the silver figures of the Cybermen trampling indifferently over the bodies strewn over the upper landing. For several seconds they were too shocked to move or speak.

'What *are* they?' Tegan finally managed to gasp, her voice a mixture of horror and fascination.

'Whatever they are they're difficult to kill . . .' muttered Scott, unable to avoid a shudder as he scanned the wreckage of the barricade and tried to assess their chances.

Tegan's fear rapidly turned into a deep and burning anger as she stared up at the mangled bodies of the dead crew members. 'Well, Lieutenant, do we go on?' she asked bluntly.

'Up there . . . past those things?' Scott snorted. 'Those poor guys were using lasers just like ours, but I don't see any of those silver things dead.'

The stairway was now clear as the Cybermen moved away along the first-level walkway and advanced towards the bridge. In a few minutes they were out of sight.

'We could at least try,' Tegan said accusingly.

Scott hesitated, filled with admiration for Tegan's plucky determination. Then he nodded and smiled. Signing to the others to follow he edged carefully out of the shadows and ran lightly towards the stairs. No sooner had they broken cover than two Cybermen suddenly appeared, returning along the walkway. Scott and his companions darted back into the shadow of the silos just in time. The two Cybermen stopped at the top of the stairs, as if guarding the route to the bridge.

'Think we could clobber those two?' Tegan whispered eagerly.

Scott crouched in the dark niche, thinking. 'There's a chance if we can all concentrate our fire,' he murmured, staring up at the seemingly indestructible figures looming above them. 'Aim at those gratings on their chests, but wait until they're facing us squarely,' he instructed.

With a thrill of excitement, Tegan primed her laser tube just as the Lieutenant had shown her and took careful aim. The whirring sound caused the two Cybermen to swing round to face them.

'Now!' Scott cried.

An intense cluster of powerful laser beams struck both Cybermen simultaneously. At first nothing happened. Then, as the Cybermen raised their deadly blasters to annihilate their attackers, thick black smoke began to pour out of their ventilator units. One of them swayed drunkenly and then overbalanced and crashed down the stairway, dropping its weapon as it fell.

'Come back here!' Scott screamed, as Tegan rushed forward. The troopers continued to fire at the Cyberman up on the walkway until it started staggering wildly about, with oily smoke and thick brown fluid erupting out of its chest. Reaching the first Cyberman, Tegan kicked its supporting arm away from under it as it attempted to get up, seized its weapon and frantically fiddled with the unfamiliar mechanism. She backed slowly against the stairway as the Cyberman succeeded in standing upright and began to advance towards her, its huge arm raised to strike.

Suddenly the blaster fired in her trembling hands. She was thrown backwards by the recoil and the Cyberman exploded in a messy hail of splinters. She sagged against the metal struts shaking violently and bathed in sweat. For a few seconds everything went blank.

Above her, the other Cyberman was lurching away towards the bridge, Scott's lasers still burning into its back.

When Tegan came to again, Scott was dragging her back into the shadows, his face a conflict of admiration and fury. 'The other one got away,' he muttered. '*We* are going back to the TARDIS.'

Despite her shocked and dazed state Tegan resisted with all her might. 'Oh no, we're not,' she retorted, shaking free, the light of battle in her eyes, 'not until we've found the Doctor and Adric.'

7

A Siege

The Doctor and Adric had been sitting morosely on the deck of the bridge, facing the wall with their hands on their heads like two naughty schoolboys. Meanwhile Briggs and Berger sat tensely at the console, fighting to keep the unwieldy old freighter stable in its warp drive. Now that the power-drain had started to subside, the Doctor was at a loss to think of some way to force the Captain to co-operate in dealing with the unknown parasitic enemy in the hold.

Eventually Adric broke an interminable silence by whispering: 'Doctor, you don't think the Captain's somehow mixed up with whatever's down in the hold?'

Before the Doctor could reply, Briggs suddenly thumped the console in exasperation. 'These surveillance monitors should be working now the power's nearly back to normal,' she complained. Most of the screens were blank although a few were blinking and strobing violently. Briggs stared at them in dismay.

The Doctor started to get to his feet. 'Perhaps I can get help,' he suggested promptly.

'You stay where you are!' Briggs snapped, flicking on the intercom. 'Ringway . . . Ringway . . . what the devil's going on?' she demanded.

There was a long and ominous silence. First Officer Berger struggled frantically with the monitor controls, while Briggs called Ringway over and over again.

Something's moving down there . . .' Ringway's shrill voice suddenly burst through before dissolving into a chaos of static. At the same moment, Berger managed to get a hazy picture on one of the monitors.

'What is it? What can you see?' Briggs shouted, thumping the intercom panel in the arm of her command seat and screwing up her eyes at the blurred but viewable image on the monitor, which showed the central section of the hold.

The intercom buzzed harshly for several seconds, but Ringway didn't reply.

'This could be it . . .' Briggs muttered grimly, gripping her chair.

'What's . . . what's *that*?' Berger's unearthly gasp made everyone look at her with a start. Then they followed her gaze to the one workable monitor. Brigg's green eyes widened and her jaw went rigid. The Doctor jumped up and followed by Adric, walked slowly towards the monitor bank, his face set in a mask of disbelief.

On the flickering screen a group of ghostly silver figures was advancing relentlessly towards the camera. A chill settled over the bridge as Berger zoomed in to show the expressionless zombie-like mask of the Cyberleader himself.

'Are these your friends, Doctor?' Briggs eventually asked in a choked voice.

'Oh most definitely not,' the Doctor breathed, his eyes fixed on the screen as if he were in a trance. Slowly he nodded his head, as if acknowledging that he should have realised something much earlier. 'Those are Cybermen,' he explained deliberately.

'Are they robots?' Adric asked incredulously.

The Doctor shook his head. 'Far, far worse,' he murmured. He turned urgently to the Captain. 'You must withdraw your crew. They don't stand a chance,' he warned her earnestly.

At that moment, Berger managed to pan the surveillance

camera to reveal Ringway's barricade starting to disintegrate under the Cybermen's deadly barrage. Then the screen flashed and went white.

Pulling off her right glove, Briggs hurried over to the armoury locker. 'Our defences are crumbling. We must go out and help,' she said defiantly.

Before she could insert her thumb into the identification lock, the access door leading to the walkway above the hold slid aside and Ringway strode onto the bridge, his laser pistol levelled. 'No, Captain, you'll stay right here,' he said coldly.

Briggs glared at him in astonishment. Then a sarcastic smile gradually creased the corners of her bright red mouth. 'The enemy's out there behind you,' she cried in scornful falsetto. 'You're pointing your laser in the wrong direction, Mister Navigator.' She whooped with laughter at her joke.

Ringway gave her a glacial smile. 'No Ma'am, I am relieving you of your command,' he crowed. 'I'm sick of your sneering and your bullying.'

The Doctor gave a short, hollow laugh. 'You haven't seen anything yet, Mister Ringway. Just wait until the Cybermen start.'

Ringway looked surprised and momentarily disconcerted. 'You know them?' he murmured.

'Oh yes, we are very old acquaintances,' the Doctor replied affably, moving slowly and casually round so as to keep Ringway's attention away from First Officer Berger standing by her seat. Through the open door behind Ringway, the sounds of the battle between the crew and the Cybermen had reached a climax. 'This slaughter is utterly pointless, you know,' the Doctor continued, keeping his piercing gaze on the nervous traitor.

'The crew is redundant,' Ringway declared flatly, keeping the Doctor covered.

'You even talk like a Cyberman,' the Doctor taunted him, aware that Berger was slowly manoeuvring herself round the end of the console.

'Those tin soldiers must be paying you an awful lot for this, Ringway,' Briggs sneered, catching the Doctor's eye.

'And I bet it isn't in *gold*,' the Doctor added significantly.

Adric had noticed that something was afoot. 'Why is that Doctor?' he asked with exaggerated curiosity.

'Because the Cybermen are highly allergic to the stuff. Suffocates them,' the Doctor explained. 'Doesn't it, Mister Ringway?'

Ringway smiled humourlessly. 'Just keep talking Doctor.'

Adric had turned away slightly and was thoughtfully fingering the large star-shaped badge pinned on his tunic.

Briggs saw that Berger had almost reached the panel on the console containing the release switches for the freighter's emergency bulkhead shutters. 'Ah . . . where do these . . . these Cybermen come from, Doctor?' she asked, forcing Ringway to follow her with his eyes as she moved beside the Doctor.

The Doctor gestured courteously to Ringway as if inviting him to answer. Ringway stared impassively back at him. 'They originally came from Mondas, but that was destroyed,' the Doctor replied. 'I'm rather surprised they didn't warn you about me, Mister Ringway.'

'Perhaps you over-estimate your own importance, Doctor,' Ringway retorted sourly.

'I doubt it. In the past I've been quite a nuisance to them . . .' the Doctor said with a cheery smile.

'What are you doing there?' Ringway shouted, suddenly suspicious of Adric's movements. Behind Ringway, Berger froze.

'Nothing,' Adric mumbled, without turning round.

Ringway lunged forward and swung the boy to face him.

85

He pressed his pistol against Adric's head and yanked his hand away from his chest. 'It's *gold*,' Ringway breathed, staring at the gleaming badge.

'Only the edge . . .' Adric protested, flinching aside so that Ringway was obliged to turn his back on the others.

Ringway ripped the star from Adric's tunic. 'Trying to conceal it, were you?' he shrieked in a strange manic tone, raising his pistol to strike.

Briggs leaped forward, chopped Ringway hard across the back of the neck and hurled him sharply against the console. At the same instant, the Doctor seized the laser from Ringway's limp hand and picked up the badge from the deck.

'Listen!' Adric murmured. There was a forbidding silence. Everyone turned towards the open doorway. 'The fighting's stopped . . .' he said.

'Quick!' Briggs yelled at Berger, who was unlocking the bulkhead-shutter master control.

At that moment, the deck began to reverberate with a heavy tramping sound and a fierce hissing. Several huge shadows suddenly fell across the landing just outside the bridge. With a gigantic crash two heavy shutters slid down over the entrances just as an enormous silver shape loomed in the doorway.

The Doctor hurried over and tapped one of the shutters dubiously. 'This won't hold them off for long,' he warned.

'They should hold until we reach Earth,' Briggs answered, flopping into her seat and surveying Ringway's motionless body with weary distaste. 'Earth Security will do the rest.'

The Doctor came over to the bank of blank surveillance monitors. 'There could be an entire invasion force,' he murmured grimly. 'How many of those silos are you carrying Captain Briggs?'

'Oh, about fifteen thousand . . .' Briggs began. She

stopped, clutching the arms of her seat in sudden horror. 'No, Doctor . . . no . . . it's not possible . . .' she stuttered.

Outside the bridge, several Cybermen were examining the material of the bulkhead shutters when their Leader strode purposefully into their midst.

'The Doctor must be taken alive,' he ordered. 'What is the delay?'

The Cyber Deputy explained what had happened.

'Our plans must not be hampered by such trivial obstacles,' the Cyberleader rasped. 'Prepare a sonic lance.'

Three of the Cybermen hastily assembled a kind of giant blowpipe. The Deputy took the sonic lance and aimed it at the centre of one of the shutters.

'Ready, Leader,' the Deputy announced.

'Excellent,' the Cyberleader boomed. 'Activate.'

A shuddering spasm ran through the device as it began to emit a low throbbing noise. Within a few seconds a dull red patch appeared in the middle of the shutter and began to spread out.

'The material is resistant, Leader,' the Deputy reported.

'More power!' the Leader ordered, and the throbbing of the sonic lance intensified.

Hissing with anticipation, the Cyberleader watched as the red glow began to brighten and to spread more rapidly over the shutter.

On the bridge, Captain Briggs was sitting motionless in her command seat staring down at Ringway's unconscious body, her lips curled in contempt. With Adric peering over his shoulder, the Doctor was pouring over computer displays showing the freighter's layout.

'We could pump all the air out of the hold,' Berger suggested, selecting a more detailed diagram of the silos.

The Doctor shook his head regretfully. 'Cybermen don't

need air, I'm afraid; in fact, they flourish in a vacuum,' he explained.

There was an agonised groan from the deck. Ringway stirred and propped his back against the front of the console.

'Pity, I've just been composing a particularly nasty epitaph for you,' Briggs muttered, jabbing Ringway with the toe of her boot. She pointed the laser pistol directly between his eyes. 'Would threatening to kill this little rat slow down those tin soldiers out there, Doctor?'

'Not in the least,' the Doctor laughed. 'They are not well known for their loyalty.'

Ringway rubbed his bruised neck. 'You're all dead already, so why don't you surrender?' he scoffed.

'I never surrender, it's too embarrassing,' the Doctor retorted, studying the computer displays closely.

Adric suddenly noticed a burning smell. Glancing round he saw the large glowing patch spreading across the shutter behind them. 'Doctor!' he shouted.

'So they've started, have they?' the Doctor murmured, hurrying over and cocking his head near the hot metal and listening. 'Sonic lance, of course,' he said to himself.

'High-frequency sound waves?' Berger exclaimed, making a half-hearted attempt to obtain a picture on the surveillance monitors.

'Probably a mixture of high and low rapidly alternating,' the Doctor explained, walking quickly round the bridge and glancing wildly at the masses of instruments as if searching for something vital.

Ringway was staring excitedly at the ominous red glow and laughing silently to himself.

The Doctor suddenly stopped and grasped Briggs's shoulder. 'You have anti-matter propulsion?' he enquired eagerly. Briggs nodded.

'Stabilised vessel containment system,' Berger confirmed.

'Excellent!' the Doctor cried, watching the spreading glow for a few seconds. 'We may be able to tap the stabiliser.'

Berger hurried over to a large panel and opened it. 'The system is controlled from this unit,' she said.

The Doctor rushed over and knelt down to peer into the unit, muttering quietly. Feeling rather superfluous, Adric went over and tried to find out what the Doctor was up to, but the Doctor simply grunted and started working busily away inside the panel.

'You're always too busy to explain anything to me!' Adric complained loudly. 'Surely I can do something . . .'

'Give me the square root of $3 \cdot 6987311$,' the Doctor shouted jumping up and striding across to the main computer terminal where he punched in some figures.

Without a pause Adric replied: 'About $1 \cdot 923209$.'

'That's impossible!' Berger cried out as the computer flashed up its answer: $1 \cdot 9232085$.

'Oh Adric's very quick,' the Doctor laughed, hurrying back to the stabiliser unit and delving back into its innards. 'You see Adric, the freighter's anti-matter fuel must be stored so that it doesn't come into contact with ordinary matter . . .'

'Otherwise they'd annihilate each other,' Adric butted in.

'Exactly,' the Doctor agreed, starting to connect one end of a long length of coaxial cable into the stabiliser. 'So this little device constantly rearranges the position of the atomic particles making up the containment vessel to keep them out of the way of the anti-particles trapped inside.'

Adric shrugged. 'But how does that help us here?'

'Simple!' cried the Doctor, 'The stabiliser will tell the atoms in the shutter that everything is all right and that they can stop letting the Cybermen's sound waves push them around.'

Adric glanced at the shutter which was now glowing bright red all over. 'But will it work, Doctor?' he murmured doubtfully.

'It's got to,' the Doctor said grimly, completing his adjustments, 'otherwise, to quote our friend Mister Ringway over there, we're all dead.'

Still sitting by Briggs's feet and covered by the laser pistol, Ringway gave a cynical laugh as the Doctor walked over to the shutter with the free end of the cable. The shutter was now a brilliant bluish-white and was beginning to sag as it started to melt.

The Doctor gave rapid instructions to Berger at the main computer and to Adric kneeling in front of the stabiliser panel. 'Now remember, Adric , when I tell you: first the red button and then the green . . .' he concluded, approaching the white-hot shutter with the cable held in his outstretched hands.

'Anti-matter . . . always hated the stuff . . .' muttered Briggs with cynical gloom, watching with a pessimistic frown as the Doctor averted his face from the searing heat and poised himself on tip-toe.

Suddenly the outline of a Cyberman pressed against the molten metal and started to force itself through the softened material. 'Now!' yelled the Doctor, lunging forward and thrusting the end of the cable against the shutter.

Adric operated the switches and Berger shrieked in terror as the huge invader tore at the shutter, shredding it like toffee. All at once the metal went cold, instantly solidifying and trapping the Cyberman like a fly in a block of amber. The cable was welded into the hard metal, connecting it permanently to the stabiliser unit.

'Bravo, Doctor!' Briggs cried delightedly, her severe features breaking into a radiant smile as she leapt to her feet.

Ringway crouched by the console, alert once more and quietly awaiting his opportunity . . .

On the other side of the shutter the Cyberleader and the Deputy surveyed the result of the Doctor's experiment with menacing calm.

'The Doctor is a formidable opponent,' rasped the Deputy, directing the sonic-lance unit to disconnect themselves.

'I anticipated as much,' the Leader hissed, striding across to the second shutter sealing the other entrance to the bridge. 'Attach diffusion charges,' he ordered, indicating the heavy shield. The Deputy began supervising the attachment of small magnetic discs in a circle round the centre of the second shield.

There was a sudden dragging sound and the Cyberman wounded by Scott and his troopers on the stairway staggered slowly round the corner from the direction of the main hold. Black smoke and steam poured out of its ventilator grille and a thick gluey fluid was oozing from its joints. A desperate rattling and whining noise emerged with each movement of its wildly jerking body.

'This unit has been damaged by laser fire!' the Deputy rasped.

'There is still resistance then,' the Leader boomed, watching the doomed Cyberman collapse in a heap and fall silent.

'The Earthling informed us that the crew totalled twenty, Leader. They have all been accounted for.'

'Then he has deceived us,' the Cyberleader hissed. 'Order the activation of reinforcements.'

The Deputy hesitated. 'But the consequences of yet further power-drains could be dangerous.'

'At once!' the Leader boomed.

The Deputy obediently tapped instructions into the communications panel on his abdomen.

'Charges primed, Leader,' announced one of the Cybermen assigned to prepare the ring of magnetic explosives.

'Activate!'

There was a rapid sequence of powerful blasts and the second shield burst inward like a paper hoop. Immediately the Cybermen raised their weapons and smashed their way onto the bridge.

Seizing his chance, Ringway knocked Briggs flying and grabbed the laser pistol.

A wry smile spread over the Doctor's face as the Cyberleader strode up to him. 'Well, at least you knocked first,' he joked, 'but I should have realised that you'd sneak in the back way.' He shot a meaningful glance at Ringway who was levelling the pistol at him, his thin face a mask of triumph.

'So we meet again, Doctor,' the Cyberleader boomed, signalling to the Deputy. The Doctor's smile instantly faded and he swallowed hard as the Deputy raised his blaster at point-blank range. Adric tried to protest, but his mouth had dried up and he managed only a bizzare kind of croak. Desperately the Doctor racked his brain for something to say to delay the awful fate only seconds away.

Slowly the Deputy turned and Ringway's victorious smile dissolved into a look of abject terror as the deadly blaster was aimed at him instead. The laser slipped from his bony hands and he started to whimper and make incoherent pleading sounds as he glanced wildly round the semicircle of impassive silver masks surrounding him. A sudden devastating bolt of energy sent him reeling against the console and his broken body slid to the deck, his face fixed in horror.

'He deceived us,' the Cyberleader explained dis-passionately.

The Cyberleader contemplated his arch-enemy in silence for a moment. 'Our records state that you have a fondness for Earth and for Earthlings,' he rasped.

'Fondness!' exclaimed the Doctor. 'I'm surprised your emotionless brain understands the word.'

'It is a word like any other, Doctor. Like "destruction". We intend to destroy your planet.'

The Doctor snorted with laughter. 'I've heard that before,' he said with a shrug.

The Cyberleader moved closer and the Doctor could not help recoiling slightly from the sweet, oily vapour that came from the ventilator grille. 'This time we shall succeed, Doctor. You will live just long enough to witness our success . . .'

Out of the corner of her eye, First Officer Berger had been watching disturbing fluctuations on the ship's instruments. 'Another power loss,' she murmured, glancing across at Briggs, who was still winded after Ringway's attack.

'Reactivation of second taskforce completed,' the Deputy announced, as a curious bleeping code sounded from his communications unit.

'Excellent,' the Leader hissed. 'Now, Doctor, you will see our strength . . .'

One of the Cybermen had been working at the controls of the bank of surveillance monitors and suddenly they flickered back into operation one after another. The Doctor, Adric, Briggs and Berger watched helplessly as the screens showed one of the silos bulging and shaking and finally tearing asunder in a twisted mass of razor-sharp slivers, like an enormous steel egg.

Out of the wrecked shell emerged more and more monstrous figures, slashing their way out of their wispy cocoons and gaining strength with each stride as they formed into a nightmare cohort of silver warriors . . .

8

War of Nerves

Down in the hold, Lieutenant Scott, Tegan and the troopers shrank into the shadows and held their breath as the shriek of slicing metal echoed around them.

'Whatever it is, it's between us and the TARDIS,' Tegan muttered, hoping that this would persuade the Lieutenant to continue the search for the Doctor and Adric, instead of retreating to the TARDIS without them.

At that moment the casing of the silo next to them started to shudder mysteriously. They scattered in all directions and hid in the niches of the neighbouring silos, watching in disbelief as the throbbing metal walls suddenly shredded and were trampled flat by the emerging Cybermen. Tegan stuffed her fist into her mouth to stifle a scream as a long wisp of plastic floated down and settled over her face like a fragment of some gigantic gossamer web. She thought she was witnessing the emergence of a swarm of loathsome silver insects, as the Cybermen flailed into life.

Clutching the captured blaster, she watched as the Cybermen formed into pairs and then dispersed along the hundreds of alleyways, their weapons poised and their deceptively blank eyes scanning the shadows relentlessly. When the juddering rhythm of their strides had subsided, she tore the clammy plastic film from her face and peered around her. Scott and the troopers had disappeared. She was quite alone.

Trying hard not to panic, Tegan cautiously began working her way along the endless rows of identical silos, darting from niche to niche in confusion, utterly unable to get her bearings. There was no sign of her friends and all around her she could hear the faint hissing and the regular tread of the Cybermen. Glancing over her shoulder she suddenly saw two of them approaching rapidly behind her. In desperation she crouched down, trying to bury herself in the floor and staring into the Cybermen's eye-pods in a vain attempt to discover whether or not they had seen her.

As they drew level she thought she was safe. Then one of them stopped and turned on her with a savage hiss. Instantly Tegan raised the blaster and fired. The Cyberman exploded and the blast sent her staggering back across the alleyway. She crashed against a silo and slumped in a daze, while the second Cyberman wrenched the blaster out of her hands and seized her arm in an unfeeling vice-like grip. Whimpering with pain, she stared mesmerised into the creature's expressionless eyes, her stomach heaving at the damp oily breath blowing into her face. For a moment nothing happened.

Then the Cyberman strode rapidly away, dragging Tegan along like a broken rag-doll . . .

As soon as the newly activated Cybermen had marched away, Scott mustered his squad and searched all around the wrecked silo for Tegan, but she was nowhere to be found.

'She must have been caught . . .' Scott muttered angrily. 'I'm to blame. I should have insisted on returning at once to the TARDIS.' He tugged his moustache nervously and hesitated.

'Perhaps the young lady's making her way there now, sir,' suggested one of the troopers.

Scott listened a moment to the eerie sounds of the Cybermen as they infiltrated the hold. 'I hope so,' he murmured. 'At least she's better armed than we are . . . but she's so headstrong.'

With every nerve alert, Scott led the squad away from

the burst silo and towards the TARDIS. As they crept along, two pairs of eyeless faces began to follow them at a distance . . .

For Nyssa and Professor Kyle, still stranded inside the TARDIS, the endless waiting had become unbearable.

'I just wish there was something positive we could do,' said Kyle, walking uncomfortably up and down in the extremely ill-fitting clothes Tegan had lent her, her arms tightly folded across her ample bosom.

Nyssa continued to fiddle with the instruments without speaking.

The Professor picked up the small radio left on the console by Scott. 'Shall we just call them . . . just to check?' she suggested in frustration for the umpteenth time.

'No,' said Nyssa, frowning at the magnetic-field indicators which were showing yet another increase. 'Try not to worry, I'm sure everything is all right.' Her voice was hollow with doubt.

Kyle glanced up at the viewer screen. 'What happens to us if the Doctor doesn't come back?' she asked quietly.

Nyssa looked up, tried to smile and shrugged.

The Professor walked slowly towards her. 'You can operate this TARDIS thing, can't you?' she demanded in a voice tinged with hysteria.

'Oh I understand most of the principles,' Nyssa replied evasively.

'But you could get us back to Earth?'

There was a pause like a chasm between them.

'Not without great difficulty,' Nyssa admitted at last, 'and even then not necessarily in the correct century.'

Professor Kyle clutched her head with bloodless fingers and gaped at Nyssa, unable to speak.

Just then, something silver emerged from the shadows on the viewer and then disappeared again.

'What was that?' Professor Kyle shrieked, pointing wildly.

Nyssa adjusted the viewer controls and zoomed in on a Cyberman motionless in the shadows. 'Those empty eyes!' she exclaimed with a shudder, staring at the huge impassive mask.

At that moment Scott and his tiny force ran into view, unaware of the alien presence lurking in the gloom.

'They'll be caught!' Professor Kyle cried, snatching up the radio again and trying to select the appropriate channel in order to warn them.

Abruptly the Cyberman turned and strode away. Seconds later there was an urgent hammering on the door of the TARDIS.

'They're safe now,' Nyssa murmured, operating the exterior door lever.

Scott burst in, followed by the troopers. Just as the last man was entering, a silver fist sliced through the open door and shattered his skull like an egg. The other troopers swung round and poured laser fire into the Cyberman's chest. After a few seconds it collapsed in a cloud of smoke. Nyssa dived at the door control just too late to prevent a second Cyberman from squeezing half-way through. Trapped by the closing door, the Cyberman discharged its blaster several times before succumbing to the concentrated laser fire burning into its ventilator unit.

Catching the full force of the blaster, Professor Kyle was hurled across the control chamber like a sack of wet sand. Her limp body hit the wall and slid to the floor with a ghastly thud. The Cyberman melted rapidly in a sparking heap.

Scott knelt beside the Professor's crumpled body. 'Professor Kyle is dead,' he said in a voice tremulous with shock.

For a moment no one moved. Then Scott pulled himself

together. 'At least we've got a chance of destroying some of those things,' he cried encouragingly, snatching up the Cybermen's discarded weapons and tossing one to one of the three surviving troopers.

'You're not going back out there?' Nyssa cried, locking the door control in the shut position.

'Earth is in grave danger,' Scott snapped resolutely. 'I have no choice. Open the door, please.'

Nyssa glanced at Professor Kyle's cruelly mangled remains. 'There has been enough bloodshed,' she murmured. 'The Doctor will not thank you for throwing away your lives.'

'Open the door!' Scott ordered.

'But the magnetic field . . .' Nyssa protested feebly.

'We've got to find the Doctor,' Scott shouted.

As the three young troopers stepped forward behind their commander, Nyssa realised that it was useless to argue. Reluctantly she opened the door. 'Good luck,' she said quietly as they hurried outside . . .

'This is sheer piracy!' Captain Briggs protested, stamping up and down her bridge in reckless indifference to the awesome presence of the Cyberleader and his forces.

'No, it is war,' the Cyberleader retorted mechanically.

'My ship is in warp propulsion mode,' Briggs continued in her high brittle voice. 'You interfere with its systems and it will disintegrate.' She nodded at the group of Cybermen engaged in removing the panelling on the console's navigation circuits.

'Your technology is primitive,' the Leader boomed. 'Mistakes will not occur.'

Briggs halted beside the Doctor. 'What the devil are they up to?' she demanded in a loud whisper.

The Doctor shook his head in despair. 'I should imagine they are locking the freighter into its present course,' he murmured. 'They are turning us into a flying bomb.'

Briggs looked as though she were about to have an apopleptic fit. She strode up to the Cyberleader and rapped sharply on his chest unit with her bony knuckles. 'You're mad if you think Earth Security will allow you and your tinny zombies to crash my ship into the planet,' she bellowed. 'They'll blow it apart long before it gets anywhere near Earth.'

The Cyberleader made a curious bubbling sound — almost as if he were giggling at the fuming little figure in front of him. 'Your ship is protected by full security clearance via the transponder,' he boomed.

'But what's the point?' Adric put in scornfully. 'On impact the anti-matter will react with matter and destroy almost everything. The planet will be useless to you.'

'That is our intention exactly,' replied the Leader. 'The Galactic Congress will be in session . . .'

The Doctor threw up his hands in contemptuous disbelief. 'So you plan to assassinate a few Galactic leaders and to destroy a beautiful planet,' he scoffed. 'Quite an achievement.'

The Cyberleader thrust Briggs aside and loomed over the Doctor threateningly. 'The Congress functions to form a military alliance against the Cybermen . . . to wage war against us.'

'A war you could not possibly win,' the Doctor said quietly.

'Exactly Doctor, their combined forces would be too powerful,' the Leader admitted calmly. 'But by striking now we shall prevent much greater conflict in the future.'

The Doctor smiled up at the huge figure and shook his head. 'Well, at least it's a welcome change from your usual war cry,' he mused ironically.

'It will be a great psychological victory for us, Doctor.

The true superiority of the Cybermen will be confirmed for ever.'

'I spoke too soon,' the Doctor muttered, turning to Adric with a grimace of disappointment. He turned back to the Cyberleader. 'So instead of your little earthquake bomb, you intend to turn the freighter into a missile.'

'Indeed, Doctor,' the Leader affirmed gravely. 'In spite of your ingenious interference, we shall succeed.'

The Doctor frowned and rocked his head very slowly from side to side as if he were trying to follow an extremely complex argument. 'But when your missile hits the Earth and explodes — aren't you and your colleagues going to be, well, rather shaken up?' he asked solemnly.

Adric could not help grinning at the Doctor's deadpan expression.

'I shall not be on board,' the Cyberleader explained with painstaking emphasis.

'Surprise, surprise!' the Doctor cried mockingly.

The Cyberleader bubbled and hissed with satisfaction. 'Your TARDIS will provide me with an excellent location from which to observe the impact, Doctor.'

The Doctor went suddenly pale. He glanced furtively at Adric. 'The TARDIS?' he said off-handedly.

'It has been found,' the Leader rasped.

'Really? I had no idea it was lost . . .' the Doctor blustered.

There was a sudden commotion in the shattered entrance.

'Doctor . . . Adric . . .' cried a familiar voice. They whirled round to see Tegan being shoved brutally onto the bridge by her captor. She wrenched herself free and ran over to them.

'Where did you spring from?' the Doctor murmured, delighted to see her, but also filled with foreboding.

'Where's Nyssa?' Adric whispered anxiously.

100

'In the TARDIS,' Tegan whispered, pushing up the sleeve of the overall and revealing a livid bruise from the Cyberman's vicious grip.

'But how did you . . .' the Doctor began, breaking off and wincing when he glimpsed Tegan's arm.

The Cyberleader strode across to Tegan and seized her bruised arm. 'Who is this?' he demanded.

'Oh . . . an Earthling. No one of any consequence,' the Doctor said quickly, suppressing his desire to smash the unfeeling robot's massive fingers with considerable difficulty.

'Oh, thanks a lot!' Tegan muttered between clenched teeth.

A curious little clicking sound could be heard somewhere inside the Cyberleader's enormous head as he stared intently at the Doctor's troubled face. 'It is clear that Time Lords have emotional feelings,' he hissed after a pause. 'Surely a serious weakness in one so rational, Doctor?'

The Doctor fumbled uncomfortably with his folded hat. 'Emotions have their uses,' he admitted reluctantly, staring at his feet.

The Cyberleader's ventilator unit bubbled with a kind of weird staccato chuckle. 'Emotions cripple the intellect,' he rasped. Tegan flinched as the oily vapour wafted into her face.

Despite all his efforts to restrain himself, the Doctor suddenly exploded with exasperation. 'Emotions also enrich life,' he retorted hotly. 'When did you last enjoy watching a sunset, or smelling the scent of flowers . . .' Instinctively the Doctor put a comforting arm round Tegan's shoulders.

'Such things are irrelevant,' the Cyberleader decreed. He thrust Tegan at arm's length. 'You feel affection for this female, Doctor?'

'She is a friend.'

'And you do not consider her friendship a weakness?'

'I do not.'

The Leader flung Tegan roughly away from them and turned to a Cyberguard. 'Kill the female!' he ordered coldly.

The Doctor screwed up his hat in anguish as he watched the Cyberman raise its blaster. Tegan said nothing, but her wide-eyed terror overwhelmed Adric, Berger and Briggs, who stood in frozen silence gazing expectantly at the Doctor. Sweat broke out on the Doctor's face as he resisted the urge to intervene and his knuckles went white. A vivid trickle of blood oozed slowly down Tegan's chin from where she had bitten her lip and the Doctor stared at the red rivulet as if transfixed.

Very, very slowly, the Cyberman's massive finger tightened on the trigger button. But still the Doctor resisted. Adric watched him incredulously, wondering whether perhaps he might even be prepared to sacrifice Tegan's life for the sake of winning this psychological struggle against the Cyberleader . . .

After what seemed like an eternity the Doctor suddenly stirred into action. 'No. Stop!' he screamed.

The Cyberleader immediately whipped up his arm, cancelling his order to destroy Tegan. 'Now you must agree that your emotions are a great disadvantage, Doctor,' he boomed triumphantly. 'I have only to threaten this female and you will obey me.'

The Doctor said nothing, but stood crestfallen and sullen, wiping the sweat from his face and taking deep relaxing breaths as he avoided Tegan's accusing stare.

The Cyberleader swung contemptuously away and, observing that the Cybermen had completed their adjustments to the circuitry inside the navigation console, strode across to Captain Briggs. 'I return your ship to you,' he announced. 'It will function entirely automatically, but you will remain on board.'

There was an ominous pause.

'But why?' Briggs demanded, glancing apprehensively at the Doctor and the others.

'That is not necessary. Let them go,' the Doctor protested.

The Cyberleader bubbled and whirred. 'And deny them the ultimate emotional experience — fear?'

The Doctor stood with bowed head, fuming at his helplessness and humiliation. 'All right, you've proved your point quite adequately,' he muttered.

The Cyber Deputy finished checking the compact device that the Cybermen had attached to the side of the console, and then marched over. 'The codes are installed, Leader. All is prepared.'

'Excellent. You will return to the control silo and inform main fleet of our revised programmes,' the Cyberleader ordered. 'All taskforce units already activated will evacuate the freighter by means of the cargo shuttle. They will rendezvous with main fleet when it arrives. You will rejoin me in the TARDIS.'

'Affirmative, Leader,' the Deputy rasped and then tramped out through the wrecked shutter.

The Cyberleader turned to his waiting minions. 'Two units will remain here to observe the behaviour of these humans under stress,' he ordered.

'Why not kill us now?' Briggs cried defiantly, her fiery little figure unflinching as she confronted the huge automaton.

'It's just sadistic,' Tegan muttered under her breath.

'Negative!' the Leader purred quietly, turning and forcing Tegan to retreat in front of him. 'It is scientific. Destruction should always be instructive. I am sure your friend the Doctor will agree. The information will be added to our data stores.'

Briggs nudged the Doctor beside her. 'Are they all so fanatically dedicated?' she murmured, casting her eyes upwards.

The Doctor grinned ruefully. 'Oh, compared to some, this chap's positively flippant,' he replied.

The Cyberleader had paused by the entrance. 'And now, Doctor, you and your female companion will accompany us to the TARDIS,' he hissed.

'The name's Tegan,' Tegan drawled scornfully.

'I shall need Adric, too,' the Doctor said quickly. 'I can't operate the TARDIS without him.

'The male remains here,' the Cyberleader grated harshly. 'We know that you alone are required to control the TARDIS.'

The Doctor shook his head and folded his arms. 'I refuse to leave without him.'

The Leader emitted a nauseating hiss, gripped Tegan by the back of the neck and shook her. 'If you do not immediately co-operate, Doctor, I shall destroy the female.' ·

There was a dangerous silence. The Doctor glanced at his two young friends in anguish.

'It's all right,' Adric said bravely. 'I'll find my own way.'

'But we can't possibly leave you,' Tegan gasped in spite of the Cyberleader's fierce grip.

Adric could bear the strain no longer. 'Doctor, please *go!*' he shouted in desperation, staring earnestly into the Doctor's troubled eyes.

'The boy's right,' Briggs chuckled stoically. 'There's still a chance for us, Doctor.'

'There is no chance,' the Cyberleader hissed, releasing Tegan.

The Doctor hesitated a moment longer. Then he slowly walked over and grasped Adric by the hand. 'Goodbye, Adric,' he murmured with a gentle smile. He stood there for a few seconds and then turned abruptly away. 'Good luck to you all . . .' he called and hurried out followed by a Cyberguard.

Adric gazed after the retreating figure and smiled weakly. 'Goodbye Doctor,' he whispered.

Close to tears, Tegan tried to speak, but she couldn't. She smiled at Adric and turned to leave.

'Goodbye, Tegan . . . I'll see you soon,' Adric said softly.

Tegan nodded and walked slowly out escorted by a Cyberman.

Framed by the jagged fragments of the exploded shield, the Cyberleader had watched the farewells with impassive concentration. He turned to the two Cybermen left guarding the bridge. 'Observe the reactions of these humans in detail . . .' he ordered gesturing at Adric, Berger and Briggs. 'They are powerless to interfere with the systems . . .'

'Affirmative, Leader,' the Cybermen rasped in unison.

Briggs shivered and sank into her command seat, pulling the wide collar of her jerkin up around her neck. 'Well, if I'm going down with my ship, at least it'll be nice to have some congenial company,' she giggled, grinning bleakly at Adric.

9

Accidents Happen

Scott and his handful of troopers were puzzled by the small number of silver automatons they had sighted after leaving the TARDIS for the second time. They had been prepared to fight every centimetre of the way, but the expected encounters had not occurred. They dodged from cover to cover among the maze of silos, expecting one of them to burst asunder at any moment and disgorge its silver horde of Cybermen. But the hold seemed almost still; as if it were waiting for something to happen.

One of the young troopers suddenly clutched Scott's arm. 'There, sir . . .' he whispered, pointing to the far end of the alleyway they were just crossing. In the distance, a large group of Cybermen were apparently walking through the side of the hold.

'Must be some kind of airlock,' Scott murmured, gripping his Cyber gun more securely and leading the way swiftly along the dark side of the alleyway towards the cluster of silver figures. When they got close, Scott motioned his squad to conceal themselves in the shadows. They watched as the last of the Cybermen entered a large cargo-port. 'They seem to be leaving the freighter,' Scott said in surprise.

'Do you think they've got the Doctor and his friends, sir?'

'Who knows?' Scott replied helplessly. 'There are far too many of them for us to go and ask!'

Just then a few stragglers marched up and squeezed themselves into the airlock. A sequence of red and amber lights flashed and the enormous shutters slowly closed behind them. There was a brief pause, followed by a sharp rush of air as the cargo-port was evacuated.

Cautiously Scott emerged from the shadows. 'Well, at least we should be able to reach the bridge now and see if we can find out what's happened to the Doctor . . .' he muttered grimly, leading the way back towards the junction near one of the wrecked silos.

Unknown to them, the Doctor was at that very moment very close. Together with Tegan, their escorts and the Cyberleader, he was making his way through the deserted hold towards the TARDIS. Ironically, the two parties passed within a few metres of each other, moving in opposite directions in the maze of walkways between the silos. The Doctor was walking along frowning silently, deep in thought, constantly fiddling with something he had concealed in his pocket.

Tegan walked beside him, blinking back her tears with great difficulty. The image of Adric's face as he bade them goodbye was printed indelibly upon her memory. Her anger surged inside her and at last it boiled over: 'You won't like Earth you know,' she snapped at the Cyberleader.

His ventilator bubbled energetically. 'Like or dislike does not enter my consideration,' he responded.

'It will once you start going rusty!' Tegan retorted crisply.

At that moment, the Cyberleader abruptly stopped beside a silo numbered 099. Tegan and the Doctor looked at each other in amazement as a curved rectangular panel opened in its wall and the Cyber Deputy emerged from the gloomy interior.

'Main fleet acknowledges your revised intentions, Leader,' the Deputy hissed efficiently.

'Excellent.'

'As soon as the freighter impacts, main fleet will

rendezvous with the secondary taskforce which has just completed embarkation in the cargo shuttle . . .'

The Doctor suddenly lunged towards the open panel. 'So this is where it all happens! *This* is your little hideaway,' he cried. 'Mind if I take a look?'

Just then the panel started to close and the Doctor was stuck half in and half out of the silo. He just caught a glimpse of the mysterious twilight within and the silhouette of the weird Cyber equipment cluttering the interior before the Cyber escort seized him by the collar and yanked him free. The panel zipped shut with a crash which echoed through the tall silo.

'Your hunger for knowledge is commendable, Doctor, but you must curb it for the present,' rasped the Cyber-leader.

With a vicious shove the escorts propelled the Doctor and Tegan on their way towards the TARDIS, while the Leader and his Deputy strode behind them with relentless mechanical steps.

But the sharp vibration of the violently slamming panel had accidentally upset the delicately balanced instruments on the main module inside the deserted silo. Unknown to the Cyberleader and his Deputy, a sequence of lights suddenly flickered on the reactivation panel and the unit began to surge into life once again, drawing power from the freighter's propulsion system and pouring it into the thousands of chrysalid Cyber units stacked abandoned in the silos . . .

With enormous effort, Nyssa had accomplished the grim and lonely task of clearing away from the control chamber of the TARDIS the bodies of Professor Kyle and the dead trooper, and the macabre wreckage of the Cyberman. Now she was trying to make sense of the readings on the console instruments, which once again warned of a huge magnetic field around the police-box.

All at once the radio Scott had left on the console bleeped urgently. Nyssa snatched it up.

'What's happening out there?' she asked nervously, her eyes glued on the console instruments.

'I don't know,' Scott answered faintly, 'It's eerie — those robot things seem to have left the ship.'

'Well, be careful, Lieutenant. That magnetic field seems to be building up again.'

'There's no sign of the Doctor and the others . . .' Scott reported, barely audibly amid the increasing buzz of static, 'but we're about to . . .' At that point his voice was completely swamped. Nyssa fiddled with the receiver, but she could not re-establish contact.

She almost jumped out of her skin when, seconds later, the exterior door swung open and the Doctor and Tegan walked in.

'Doctor . . . Tegan . . .' she exclaimed in delighted relief, barely managing to retrieve the radio before it slipped out of her fingers to the floor. The brilliant smile was immediately wiped from her fine features as the towering figures of the Cyberleader and the Deputy strode through the door.

'It's a shambles,' muttered Tegan, 'an absolute shambles.'

The Doctor threw Nyssa a brief, shamefaced glance as he crossed to the console. He closed the exterior door and then started working feverishly away at preparations for departure.

'Where's Adric?' Nyssa asked, smuggling the small radio unit onto the console behind her. She backed away as the Deputy advanced ominously around the console towards her.

'Safe,' replied the Doctor evasively, without looking at her.

A moment later there was a hideous scraping noise and the TARDIS creaked and wobbled alarmingly as it de-materialised from inside the hold. The Cybermen's rigid faces betrayed no reaction as the craft shuddered and shook before gradually stabilising again as it materialised outside the hull of the freighter. A few seconds later, the freighter's gigantic bulk flickered into view on the screen.

'There,' the Doctor mumbled. 'We are locked onto the freighter's co-ordinates.'

'Excellent,' boomed the Cyberleader, who had been watching the Doctor's activities at the console closely. He turned abruptly to the Deputy. 'Search the TARDIS,' he ordered.

'What are those things doing here?' Nyssa demanded, turning angrily to the Doctor as the Deputy marched out through one of the internal doors.

'We shall observe the collision of the freighter with Earth and the planet's final destruction,' the Leader hissed.

At this, Tegan flared up. 'You'll ruin your own plan,' she shouted. 'Earth surveillance radar will pick up the TARDIS!'

The Cyberleader bubbled and whirred quietly. 'the TARDIS is not radar-reflective,' he retorted, consulting the chrono-disc built into his forearm. 'The time draws near . . . our victory is imminent.'

Tegan gritted her teeth and glared hard at the Doctor as if he were responsible. 'Doctor, can't you do *anything*?' she cried, her pale face creased with grime and exhaustion.

'Not just at the moment,' he replied in an undertone.

'Do not mislead the Earthling,' the Cyberleader boomed. 'You can do nothing now Doctor.'

Suddenly Tegan went absolutely wild. Before anyone could restrain her she threw herself onto the console. 'I don't have to stand by and watch my planet being destroyed . . .' she screamed, flailing madly at the controls. The TARDIS immediately started to shudder convulsively, tilting this way and that and emitting howls of protest from deep within its mechanism.

110

The Cyberleader snatched Nyssa by the arm and thrust his blaster brutally against the side of her head.

'Stop it, Tegan, stop it!' the Doctor yelled, frantically grabbing hold of her and struggling to drag her away from the console. But Tegan clung on, screaming and fighting, while Nyssa began to whimper with pain and terror. Eventually the Doctor managed to twist Tegan round so that she could see Nyssa's plight as the Cyberleader threatened her with instant disintegration.

Gradually Tegan calmed down, and went limp and quiet. The Doctor held her firmly with one hand while he readjusted the controls with the other. Soon the TARDIS had steadied and settled into its familiar contented humming.

'You do things like that and we'll all finish up dead in no time at all,' he whispered into her ear, hugging her tightly.

Slowly the Cyberleader released Nyssa's arm. It had been gripped so tightly that her hand was a livid chalky white and totally numbed.

The Leader surveyed them with intense concentration, as if he were watching some extraordinary experiment. 'Fascinating,' he hissed. 'What a fascinating species . . .'

On the bridge of the freighter, Adric and First Officer Berger were standing on either side of Captain Briggs, who was slumped gloomily in her command seat. The trio were talking in low voices, out of earshot of the two Cybermen standing guard over them at the entrance. Adric had been surreptitiously eyeing the complex little device which the Cybermen had connected into the navigation circuits earlier. It consisted of a rack containing three sets of small discs all of which were capable of rotating relative to one another and forming different combinations.

'Any chance of undoing whatever that is?' Briggs murmured quietly.

111

'How much time have we got?' Adric whispered.

'Not long. We're on full warp drive,' Berger answered.

Adric glanced across at the Cybermen. 'Given time, I'm sure I could do something,' he murmured. Even if we diverted the ship only a few degrees, we'd still miss Earth by a safe margin. But we'd have to do it soon.'

'We'd also have to divert our two knights in shining armour a lot more than a few degrees first,' Briggs muttered sceptically.

The fluorescent lighting concealed in the ceiling had been fading for some time and now there was a sudden spasmodic flicker. One of the Cybermen went over to the console.

'There is a power malfunction,' it grated, adjusting some controls.

Adric and the others tensed and held their breaths, ready to seize their opportunity should it arise. But the second Cyberman was still aiming its blaster directly at them. 'That is not possible,' it hissed. 'Reactivation has been cancelled.'

At that moment, Adric glimpsed a familiar figure framed in the debris of the exploded shutter behind the second automaton.

It was Lieutenant Scott. Just as Scott put his finger to his lips, a fierce burst of blaster fire sounded from the main hold. The two Cybermen both turned just as Scott stepped through the hole onto the bridge. Adric dived behind the end of the console, dragging Briggs and Berger with him, a split second before Scott fired his blaster, hitting the Cybermen with a devastating fusillade of sonic pulses which shook them to pieces, their outer casings collapsing as if the inside had turned to jelly.

'Where's the Doctor?' Scott shouted as he heaved the smoking wreckage of one of the Cybermen off the console.

With the ominous sounds of battle getting louder from the direction of the main hold, Adric explained in a few

112

hasty sentences exactly what had been happening, while Briggs knelt and tugged at the panels protecting the navigation circuits.

Berger had already tried to key new instructions into the guidance computer. 'It's no good, my instructions are instantly countermanded,' she cried despairingly.

'That's our problem there,' Adric informed the Lieutenant, pointing to the disc rack, 'but I think it can be disconnected if I could solve the three logic codes . . .'

There was another prolonged burst of laser and blaster fire from outside.

'That could take you forever,' Berger objected. 'The combinations must be almost infinite.'

'And the thing's probably booby-trapped,' Briggs warned.

'Then I'd better start at once!' Adric cried, peering closely at the weird device on his hands and knees.

One of the troopers rushed onto the bridge, 'Lieutenant, those silver things . . . they're breaking out of those containers . . . the hold's crawling with them and the lasers are almost finished,' he panted.

'I'm coming,' Scott shouted, tossing him the two blasters abandoned by the two wrecked Cybermen. 'We'll hold them off as long as we can!' he called over his shoulder to Adric before rushing out behind the trooper.

Adric knelt by the device and very carefully started moving the discs on the top set around. He knew that the possible combinations totalled several billions, but he guessed that there would be patterns of more likely sequences — if only he could use his formidable mathematical ability to work them out in time.

'Power seems to be fully restored again,' Berger reported after a few minutes. 'We seem to be going faster than ever now . . .'

Out on the walkway above the main hold, Scott and his squad had managed to rebuild a sort of makeshift fortification out of the debris left by Ringway's crew earlier. From behind it they did their best to pick off the newly activated Cybermen as they emerged from among the silos below them. In the centre of the huge hold, several silos had burst open and wave upon wave of gleaming automatons were advancing on the stairway. They seemed intent on revenge, as if they somehow knew that they had been abandoned by their masters and had only been reactivated by accident.

These Cybermen did not seem to be as powerful as the previous attackers, as if their reactivation had been premature or incomplete. Pieces of them flew everywhere as they marched unsteadily into the concentrated barrage of blaster fire unleashed by Scott and his troopers and the air was filled with smoke, sparks and streams of oily fluid. Gradually, however, their retaliation grew stronger, and more and more of them began reaching the stairway before being sent reeling by the defenders behind the barricade. Little by little, the troopers found themselves being forced to retreat back along the walkway towards the bridge . . .

With the horrifying sounds of the battle for the walkway growing louder every minute, Adric darted backwards and forwards between the Cyber device and the main computer, desperately struggling to solve the complex algebraic combinations.

'Are you sure that's right?' Berger queried doubtfully as he tapped some figures into the input.

'It has to be. It's the only logical answer,' Adric murmured, watching the print-out anxiously. There was a long pause. Then, at last, a long series of symbols chattered out.

'That's it!' Adric yelled joyfully. 'The first code is solved!' He knelt down and feverishly adjusted the discs on the first of the three tiers of combinations. There was a hum and then a sharp click. 'Yes, it's worked. See if it's released anything.'

'We're running out of time,' Briggs muttered darkly. 'Your friends won't be able to hold off those silver dummies much longer.'

'Stand by!' Berger called out, gradually easing the navigation controls slightly, her face furrowed with apprehension. Nothing happened. Biting her lip, she eased them a little further. Still nothing happened. With a fearful glance at Adric and Briggs she moved them more and more . . .

All at once a deafening howl ran through the freighter and it tilted violently, sending them all skidding across the sloping deck and into the rear wall. The gigantic craft vibrated as if it were going to shake itself to pieces and the noise was so loud that Adric could not hear what Berger and Briggs were screaming at him, although their faces were almost touching his. All three tried to crawl back up the steep slope towards the console, but the deck was far too slippery and an overwhelming centrifugal force seemed to be crushing them down.

'I can't . . . I can't move . . .' Adric gasped, fighting for breath.

As the dreadful howling reached a climax, they stared helplessly up at the warning lights that flashed urgently all over the console, until the irresistible force drove their heads against the cold metal floor.

In the hold, the Cybermen had just begun to gain ground, trampling heedlessly on their fallen as they surged up the stairway and onto the walkway above. As the freighter went out of control, the troopers were thrown forward against their makeshift barricade; but the Cybermen were completely disorientated: they staggered and slid all over the place and then lay immobilised, their electro-gyroscopic balancing mechanisms utterly ineffective. The troopers saw

115

Scott's mouth opening and shutting in his contorted face as he tried to shout orders to them, but no sound penetrated through the cataclysmic roaring and buffeting of the shuddering spacecraft . . .

The Doctor, Nyssa and Tegan watched in silence as the image of the freighter faded and reappeared and faded again on the viewer in the TARDIS control chamber.

'What's happening, Doctor?' Nyssa exclaimed, as the flickering grew faster and faster.

In a few seconds the freighter's image had disappeared altogether.

'Where's it gone?' Tegan cried, her voice breaking with tension.

'The freighter seems to have entered a warp spiral,' murmured the Doctor mysteriously. 'It's going backwards.'

The Cyberleader raised his blaster. 'You will follow, Doctor,' he ordered.

The Doctor's eyebrows shot up. 'Follow?' he snorted. 'Where?'

'Follow them . . .' the Cyberleader rasped threateningly, 'You will rematerialise the TARDIS on board the freighter.'

'That's quite impossible!' the Doctor protested, as the image of the huge craft reappeared on the screen for a second and then promptly faded again. 'I've got nothing to lock on to. The freighter's co-ordinates are randomly fluctuating — that's why it keeps fading.'

The towering automaton emitted a sharp, oily sigh. 'You will do as I command, Doctor.'

The Doctor shrugged. 'I've already told you . . .' he stalled.

Tegan glared defiantly at the Cyberleader. 'Well, if the freighter's going backwards now — the Earth must be safe,' she butted in.

The Doctor glanced at the instruments on the console and then shook his head regretfully. 'I'm sorry, Tegan, although the freighter is spiralling backwards in *time*, I'm afraid it's still following the same *spatial* vectors,' he pointed out quietly.

On the viewer, the freighter reappeared faintly.

'Towards Earth . . .?' Tegan asked lamely. The Doctor nodded.

The Cyberleader bubbled with satisfaction. 'Excellent, Doctor, Earth will therefore be destroyed long before it ever existed in the form you have known it,' he purred.

Tegan turned to the Doctor, tears welling in her eyes. 'Is that true?' she murmured incredulously.

'It is entirely possible . . .' the Doctor admitted ambiguously.

Just then, the freighter's image had stabilised on the screen and it was now sharply in focus again. Far beyond it, among the brilliant background of stars filling the rest of the viewer, a tiny bluish-white disc had appeared and was slowly growing larger.

'Earth . . .' the Doctor whispered, almost reverently.

Speechless, Nyssa and Tegan watched the beautiful, serene planet glowing in the sunlight.

'Excellent. Hold this position, Doctor,' the Cyberleader ordered, with a hiss of anticipation. 'We shall observe the impact from here.'

Studiously avoiding his young friends' accusing stares, the Doctor gazed at the screen, his hands thrust deep into his jacket pockets. His fingers eventually closed round something sharp and metallic which had been lying there forgotten: the gold-rimmed star awarded to Adric for Mathematical Excellence. Every now and then, the Doctor glanced out of the corner of his eye at the console displays which showed how far back in time the freighter

117

was taking the TARDIS as it hurtled inexorably towards the Earth.

Gradually, the faintest of smiles began to flicker around the Doctor's mouth . . .

10

Triumph and Tragedy

With the memory of the freighter's ominous death-howl still ringing in their ears, Adric, Briggs and Berger hauled themselves groggily to their feet as the cumbersome ship slowly righted itself again and the vibrations died away.

'I feel as if I've been walked on by an entire army!' Briggs complained, following the other two over to the console. 'What happened?'

'We accelerated into a time spiral,' Berger exclaimed, quickly checking the displays. 'We've travelled backwards in time . . .' she added in astonishment.

'But that's impossible!' Briggs laughed, after a stunned silence.

'Don't you believe it!' Adric said, tackling the solution of the second logic code on the main computer.

At that moment Scott ran onto the bridge, followed by his three surviving troopers who formed a battered and exhausted semicircle round the entrance, their blasters aimed at the walkway outside.

'That was some bump!' Scott panted. 'What happened?'

Briggs sank into her command seat, staring apprehensively at Adric and Berger who worked feverishly away at the computer. 'Don't even ask,' she sighed, in a drained voice. She punched a series of buttons in the arm of the seat and a brilliant star-field flashed onto the main navigation monitor. In the very centre of the screen glowed the Earth. 'Anyway it hasn't made the slightest difference,' she muttered hopelessly, gesturing up at the screen. 'We're still bang on course.'

Adric frowned hard at the long sequence of numbers

rapidly appearing on the computer display. Then he darted over to the code racks attached to the side of the navigation system and swiftly revolved the discs on the second set. There was a hum followed by a pause and then a sharp click.

'That's it. The second logic code should be released now!' he cried, waving excitedly across to First Officer Berger.

Berger immediately responded at the controls. There was an anxious silence while she checked her instruments. Meanwhile Scott joined his troopers on guard at the entrance, listening for the merest hint that the Cybermen had recovered from the freighter's temporary upheaval.

At last Berger clapped her hands. 'We've come out of warp propulsion mode!' she announced delightedly. 'It's working, Adric!'

Adric wiped the sweat from his eyes. 'Only one more code to crack,' he grinned, returning to the computer terminal.

Suddenly Scott swung round. 'I think they're coming . . .' he warned. The troopers backed away from the entrance a little.

Briggs stood up. 'There's nothing more we can do,' she said, striding across the bridge to the emergency escape-pod hatch. She removed her glove and inserted her thumb into the identification lock. 'Abandon ship!' she ordered.

'This is your planet that's in danger you know!' cried Adric accusingly as he crouched over the computer keyboard, frantically trying to solve the last of the three codes.

'I am well aware of that, young man,' Briggs snapped icily, 'but in a few minutes from now we shall enter Earth's gravitational field and we are still fixed on a direct collision course.'

With a soft buzzing sound the emergency airlock opened.

'There's still time to crack the third code,' Adric protested. 'It's much more complex, I admit, but . . .'

'Abandon ship!' Briggs repeated, raising her voice in a kind of swooping falsetto.

Adric glanced at the monitor. The Earth was looming

larger and larger. Berger came over and gently took him by the arm. 'Adric, you've done all you can,' she said.

Reluctantly, Scott ordered his troopers into the airlock. 'Hurry, lad,' he urged, as Adric resisted Berger's persuasive grasp.

'Just one more minute . . . please . . . I know I can do it!' Adric pleaded.

'That's an order!' Scott insisted.

Adric allowed himself to be led across to the airlock where Captain Briggs was ushering everyone through the hatch. She stood aside, gesturing to Adric to join the others in the escape capsule while she cast a final glance around the bridge she had commanded for so long. As he entered, Adric's sharp eye noticed the irreversible initiation control fitted into the wall at the capsule end of the airlock.

When Briggs eventually stepped into the capsule, Adric slipped out past her, tapping the initiation button as he went. Before Briggs could react, the airlock doors had started to close. Adric waved at the startled and horrified faces and just caught a glimpse of Briggs's severe face as she mouthed 'Good luck' at him a split second before the airlock sealed itself shut between them.

'Don't worry. I'll be all right!' he shouted.

Alone on the deserted bridge, Adric ran across to the computer and resumed work on the fiendishly complicated calculations. Above his head, the Earth now almost entirely filled the monitor. 'I can do it . . . I can do it . . . I must do it . . .' he murmured over and over again, as if he were uttering some kind of magic incantation.

So engrossed was he that he failed to hear the sinister shuffling and hissing sounds coming closer and closer along the walkway. In his excitement he had forgotten all about the Cybermen . . .

Nyssa watched the viewer with bated breath as the tiny silver capsule slowly pulled away from the huge dark hull of the freighter. For a moment she was filled with hope. 'What is it?' she murmured.

Tegan moved beside her and clasped her hands anxiously together. 'Adric?' she whispered, turning expectantly to the Doctor.

'My secondary taskforce is evacuating the freighter,' boomed the Cyberleader. 'We shall complete the destruction of any surviving systems or life-forms on Earth following the explosion of the freighter.'

The Doctor frowned at the images of the capsule, the freighter and the Earth on the viewer. 'Oh, I wouldn't be too sure about that,' he retorted, glancing signficantly at his two friends as he drew his hands out of his pockets and clasped them firmly behind his back. 'It may interest you all to know that we have reversed our time co-ordinates by some sixty-five million years.'

The Cyberleader emitted a hot, rancid hiss and rapidly scanned the instruments on the console as if trying to check the truth of the Doctor's startling announcement.

'Big deal, Doctor,' Tegan sniffed.

'Just think about it,' the Doctor continued earnestly. 'Remember the fossil dinosaur bones in the cavern?'

'And the reason the dinosaurs died out so suddenly!' Nyssa added excitedly, pointing to the viewer screen.

'So what?' Tegan shrugged impatiently, more concerned with the fate of Adric than the history of the dinosaurs. 'Everybody knows that the Earth collided with some kind of . . .' She stared at the viewer wide-eyed for several seconds, her jaw dropping. 'The freighter?' she exclaimed with a gasp. '*That*'s the "asteroid"?'

The Doctor nodded. 'It is inevitable now. The anti-matter containment vessel will burst open on impact, with a colossal explosion,' he explained, with a reassuring smile. 'The history of your planet is secure after all. Thanks to the Cybermen!'

The Cyberleader rounded on the Doctor with a menacing rasp. 'You lie, Doctor . . .' he roared, stamping across the chamber and looming over the smiling Time Lord.

The Doctor backed away very slowly. 'Not at all. You have lost. The Earth is safe and the Congress will proceed as planned — in approximately sixty-five million years' time!' he cried, with a mocking laugh, spreading his clenched fists wide in an expansive gesture of defiant satisfaction.

At that moment, the small radio lying on the console bleeped urgently and Nyssa snatched it up.

Scott's voice crackled faintly from the speaker. 'Scott to the TARDIS . . . Scott to the TARDIS . . .'

'This is the TARDIS,' Nyssa hurriedly replied, 'we have Cybermen on board and . . .'

Before she could say any more, the Cyberleader had wrenched the radio out of her slender hand.

Scott's voice crackled on: 'We've managed to escape from the freighter, but I'm afraid Adric is still aboard . . .'

The Lieutenant's words abruptly ceased as the Cyberleader's enormous hand crushed the radio into a mess of wires and transistors and dropped the debris onto the floor.

'So Adric's still trapped,' Tegan gasped in a choked voice, her eyes brimming with tears as she stared up at the image of the freighter on the viewer. 'We've all failed him.'

The Doctor had been smiling ironically at the mangled remains of the radio, filled with contempt for the Cyberleader's puny gesture of superiority. 'I fear that the Cybermen have failed yet again,' he said quietly.

The Cyberleader swept Nyssa aside with a savage thrust and advanced on the Doctor with his blaster directed straight at the Doctor's head. 'A temporary setback to our plans, Doctor,' he hissed, 'but you will not be in a position to celebrate any victory against us.' The massive automaton stopped a metre away from his old adversary, the deadly blaster only centimetres from his victim's face. 'For you the end has come, Doctor . . .'

Nyssa and Tegan stared helplessly at the Doctor's ashen face. Then Tegan suddenly caught a glimpse of something she recognised glinting between the Doctor's fingers. Instantly she shoulder-charged the towering Cyberleader with all her strength. Her slight frame bounced off his gigantic bulk like a pingpong ball, but the Cyberleader was distracted just long enough for the Doctor to leap forward and manoeuvre himself round behind the cumbersome figure. Flinging both arms around the Cyberleader's thick body, he was able to scrape the gold edge of Adric's badge rapidly up and down the serrated grille covering the ventilator unit on the automaton's chest.

Immediately the precious but deadly grains were sucked into the unit. Nyssa and Tegan dived for cover beneath the console as the Leader's blaster fired erratically in all directions as he swung violently from side to side in a vain attempt to throw the Doctor off. The Doctor cried out in agony as the Leader trapped his forearms between metal elbows and armoured sides. But still he rubbed the badge as hard as he could against the grille, and more and more gold filings were sucked into the ventilator.

Gradually the Cyberleader began to emit a desperate choking sound and sticky black bubbles started frothing out of the grille. Tegan threw herself in a kind of rugger tackle at the monster's legs and clung on for dear life as the thing staggered wildly about, whipping viciously to and fro and firing the blaster haphazardly at the console and the walls of the chamber as it struggled to maintain its balance.

Eventually the Cyberleader's movements became more and more sluggish and his cries more and more like the sound of a human being fighting for breath. Finally he slumped forward and the Doctor took his chance to grab the blaster from the Cyberleader's weakening grasp. Yelling to Tegan to

124

let go of the legs, the Doctor thrust the weapon against the Cyberleader's unit and fired repeatedly until its voice faded into silence. It stood stiffly to attention for a moment and then crashed to the floor in a spectacular shower of sparks.

At once the Doctor turned to the damaged console and began frantically trying to repair the section hit by the blaster.

Nyssa helped Tegan to her feet. 'Doctor, please hurry. We must get Adric off the freighter,' she pleaded.

The Doctor shook his head helplessly and gestured at the shattered instruments.

'Please, Doctor, we must save him . . .' Tegan cried, turning to the viewer. The Earth almost filled the entire screen.

'I'm sorry. There's too little time,' the Doctor murmured. 'Any moment now the freighter will enter Earth's atmosphere. Nothing can stop it now.'

Adric stood alone on the bridge, staring blankly at the last calculations still remaining to be solved before the third logic code could be broken. However hard he puzzled, the complex mass of figures on the fluorescent screen made no sense whatever to him.

'There's something I've forgotten,' he murmured, absently fingering the torn threads of his tunic where his Mathematical Excellence Badge had been ripped off. 'Something simple but vital I've left out of the matrix . . .'

Above his head, the main observation monitor was entirely filled with the soft blues, greens and greys of the Earth's swiftly approaching surface. Adric could not help allowing the awesome beauty of the serene planet to distract him for several seconds. When he turned his attention back to the computer display, a sudden obvious error was staring him in the face.

'Of course . . . that's it!' he cried, immediately tapping a fresh set of figures onto the keyboard with feverish haste.

'It's just the reciprocal group of the logarithmic. How could I have been so stupid?'

At that moment, a harsh roar made him spin round. He just had time to glimpse a huge silver shape looming in the entrance and to hurl himself aside before a burst of energy blasted the computer keyboard into a hunk of fused metal. He cowered behind the command seat, sucking his throbbing fingers and staring in frozen terror at the wounded Cyberman swaying drunkenly and trying vainly to aim its blaster at him.

Gradually the Cyberman toppled forward onto its face, exuding a kind of black oily pus from its shattered joints and lay still. Adric scrambled back to the console and gazed for a long time at the utterly useless keyboard. Then he looked up at the huge, luminous image of the Earth rushing towards him and a wry smile spread across his calm round face.

'And now I'll never know if I was right . . .' he murmured, shivering slightly as if a sudden chill had swept through the bridge, although the instruments were indicating a massive temperature increase in the freighter's structure.

Then he folded his arms very tightly around his body as if to comfort himself and stood waiting quietly for the end which he knew could only be seconds away . . .

Meanwhile, assisted by Nyssa, the Doctor was desperately fighting to regain control of the TARDIS, which had been thrown out of equilibrium by the Cyberleader's blaster fire. 'We must save Adric . . .' he gasped, leaning against the jammed levers with all his weight, like an old-fashioned aviator trying to force his biplane out of a crash-dive.

The TARDIS shuddered and groaned, but refused to respond. 'It's no good,' the Doctor cried, shaking the sweat out of his eyes and glancing at Nyssa in desperation. 'I can't shift her . . .'

Nyssa added her modest weight to the immovable controls, but they remained completely stuck.

Armed with twisted fragments of Adric's gold-rimmed badge, Tegan had positioned herself behind an interior door to await the return of the Cyber Deputy from his tour of inspection. With thumping heart, she stared up at the viewer which showed the freighter's hull already beginning to glow a dull red from the friction of the Earth's atmosphere as the doomed craft plummeted towards the surface.

'Please, Doctor . . . please hurry . . .' she whispered to herself over and over again, still hoping against hope that the Doctor might succeed in making a last-minute attempt to rescue Adric.

Suddenly the door flew open and the Cyber Deputy strode back into the chamber. At once Tegan ducked out of the way of his powerful arms and started scraping the gold edge of Adric's badge as hard as she could against the grille of his ventilator unit. With one enormous hand the huge automaton clawed frantically at its chest, while with the other it struggled to operate the trigger mechanism of its blaster. Evil yellow and black bubbles poured out of the ventilator as the stricken Deputy fought against the deadly dust, rattling and gasping in desperation. Tegan dodged about, forcing the flaking gold slivers into the grille with all the strength she could muster.

Seizing the blaster captured from the Cyberleader earlier, the Doctor yelled a warning to Tegan. As she rolled to safety under the console, he fired a long and devastating salvo which quickly reduced the Cyber Deputy to a buckled wreck. The sparking automaton crashed to the floor beneath a pall of greasy smoke and lay motionless.

Tegan scrambled breathlessly to her feet and gazed up at the viewer. She tried to say something, but she could only point silently at the terrible image on the screen. The freighter was glowing an intense blue-white which was almost unbearable to look at.

Throwing down the blaster, the Doctor hurried over and

127

put his arms round Tegan and Nyssa. Together they watched helplessly the final moments of the incandescent missile, their faces as pale and immobile as plaster masks.

Suddenly a brilliant flash seared their eyeballs as the freighter exploded into a molten cascade of tiny fragments. Then the screen went completely black, as if the stars had abruptly been extinguished. A few seconds later, the TARDIS was shaken by a series of sharp jolts as the shock wave reached it. From the console came a number of quiet clicks as the jammed controls freed themselves.

No one spoke as the Doctor and his two companions watched the glorious patterns of the heavens gradually reappear on the viewer, shimmering silently in the infinite emptiness.

After a while, the Doctor went over to the wreckage of the Cyber Deputy and dislodged what was left of the metal star from the ventilator grille. He stared at it in the palm of his hand for a moment. All the gold edging had vanished.

With a sad smile he dropped it into his pocket and turned resignedly towards the console . . .